THE UNMOVING SKY

K. L. HALLAM

Dedicated to Sojourner and Aeon

CONTENTS

❧   I   ❧

Artie sure is fast on his feet. Even wet grass can't slow him down. What he lacks in physical strength, he makes up for in agility. I'm the one who tends to slip. Only this time I catch myself before I'm flat in the mud.

"Artie, where you going?"

"Remember the shortcut? Mom used to tell us to follow the trillium flowers if we ever got lost." The small white flowers, promising spring, wind along the creek through to Mr. Potters, are at risk of disappearing if not protected."

"Wait—hold up."

I meet with Artie at the edge of the ravine. The white flowers line the creek and wind their way upstream. Artie stares out over the drop, the cold wind whipping his uncut curls against his face. He looks so much like Mom, and so far away.

"What's wrong?" I ask before he disappears completely.

It takes a minute for Art to figure out what to say. I know he's thinking about her. "Ah, nothing." He shakes his head and turns from the ravine.

He knows I know.

And like that, I let it be. There's an understanding between us, a secret language we've had to use to conceal our communication when our father's around. Rick has little time for goofing off or carrying on, not from us or anyone else.

We hike back through the thicket of bare branches, through the buds on the verge of bursting open for the new spring. My breath floats in waves and surrounds me. Somehow I've gotten ahead of Artie. I turn to see if he's listening since I've been talking on and on. If Artie's the quiet one, I'm the rambler. Mostly I note the species of plants we pass. It keeps my head occupied, keeps me from the negative thoughts and feelings that are about to hit me across the face when we get back. There'll be a message from Bri, and about a hundred on my phone that I can't check without reception. She'll have to talk to Rick. But that's something she does better than me. Even if we do our best to avoid him when she's around.

In the meantime, I keep an eye on Artie. I'm the older brother. Mom told me to watch over him, knowing Rick would have other things on his mind. Or be completely unavailable. Artie's my responsibility. He's three years younger, but some days I feel way older, like an old man, really, and only seventeen —a whole year from official adulthood. But I know responsibility.

I went with Brianna, last September, held her hand, stood by her side. She had that look on her face: serene and patient, at peace with the decision. A decision we made together. That was also my responsibility. It's not as if I'd leave her when she needed me most. Not the way Rick left us.

But I'm not sure how I feel anymore. If I stay with Brianna out of guilt, or I'm waiting until she breaks up first. She knows I've been avoiding her phone calls.

I JUST NEED TIME AWAY, time to think, figure out what comes next. If we have a future, or we go through the motions until one of us breaks? Breaks down or breaks away. Isn't that what everyone expects.

~

A HAZE of grey covers everything. The rainy season, but should more accurately be called the mud season. The brown flows where the water flows. Artie and I meet again at the creek, now a small brook lined with bluebells, and walk north. We continue heading upstream until we spot the hunting lodge. With the chimney pumping out puffs of warm smoke, the lodge looks inviting. But it's not.

Rick never notices we're gone. It's half past six-pack time, and maybe 3:00 in the afternoon. I know his drinking schedule pretty well. If he hasn't shot anything today he'll drink his weight in beer, and take his frustrations out on me, and Artie. That's why I can't leave. One wrong word from him and Artie slips away further and if Rick were to ever lay a hand on him—that's something I can't allow myself to think about. Since as far as I know that hasn't happened yet.

Brianna has nothing weighing on her now. She can go off to college focused.

Rick doesn't "get" Artie. He really doesn't. I play along sometimes with all the dude stuff. But Artie doesn't care. He does what he feels, and he's got big ideas. Mom used to say Artie was a dreamer. I think our father takes this as weakness — and Artie's weakness is his fail.

We trudge through the mud, each step sticks to our boots. Artie laughs as we almost fall out of our shoes. A blue jay's lonely call cries out.

The sky hovers low, without a streak of depth. The kind of grey morning we lost Mom. And Rick Bower wasn't there. He wasn't there to console Artie. It was only me. Me, and the nurses we hardly knew, hovering over her limp body.

The front door of the lodge swings open.

"Jackson! Where the hell have you two been?"

Artie gets that expression of his. His eyes dart over to me, he steps a few paces back.

"I got this," I whisper to him.

Rick holds a can of beer. No gun. He isn't happy.

"We were following some bear tracks," I lie. Out looking for bears, is something I say to keep his mood stable. But there's very little you can hide from a cop, even an intoxicated one.

He doesn't respond and empties his last swig of beer. "Well, come on, your lunch is cold." He retreats indoors, and doesn't hold the door, or wait. Artie curls a smile at me and walks ahead.

Inside, Mr. Gallows and Pete Winger sit at a table, playing poker with a couple of new guys. I can't remember their names. I thought Rick let us pass without much altercation. I guess there is safety in numbers — our safety.

Rick has already joined them, asking to be dealt in. Art and I are hungry. We leave our hiking boots by the door and replace them with house sneakers. Looks like everyone's having hamburgers. Again. There isn't anything for Artie to eat. He knows Artie's a vegetarian now, but he likes to ignore that small fact. Artie's good at getting by on sides: side of chips, side of pickles, not a very good lunch. When Mom was healthy she was a great cook. Rick's idea of vegetables is pickles and onions, stuff he can throw on a sandwich.

"That girl called for you," Rick says.

"Brianna?" He knows her name.

"Uh-huh." He snorts.

I haven't seen her in almost two weeks. The longest we've been apart since we started going out a year ago. No telling when Rick plans on driving back to Gravelsburg. I expect we'll stay out here for the entire break. I'm at his mercy without a car of my own. Got so used to Brianna driving everywhere and feel somewhat stranded out here, holding Artie and myself barely above water. But we need this time apart.

Brianna reaching out gets under my skin, a sort of agitation, or is it impatience? I have a sudden urge to know what's on her mind.

"I'll call her back on the landline. Catch any turkeys?"

I want to ask if they caught any bears, but if they didn't I'd just get a lot of slack for asking. They talked a big game last night. He might think I'm goading him. I keep my mouth shut. The bigger the game the greater their thrill, I suppose. There's little I can say to change their decades-old habit. But maybe Artie will, one day.

"Hell, yeah. Look out back," one of the "unknowns" says.

I glance out the window and focus about twenty meters away, where five or more turkey carcasses hang on the line. "We might get some coyotes in on the action," I mention, surprised they weren't already.

"Naw, Gunner's watching the birds," Mr. Gallows says. "I raise you."

I wonder how that shepherd-mix can contain himself? Suppose there're dire consequences if he doesn't.

I look back at Artie. He makes a face of disapproval at the turkeys hung by their feet. Blood drips into the mud underneath.

I grab a hamburger. Slices of soggy, unripe tomatoes sit on a plate, and there're a few offerings of sandwich fixings. Artie's so used to the drill, he makes a salad from the lettuce, the onions, and tomatoes, and places the pickles Art-fully on top. That's Artie. He knows how to make do.

The phone rings.

"It's probably your girlfriend again, who else would call out here?" Rick says.

He's right about that. I pick up the phone in the kitchen and hesitate when I realize my hand is shaking. What's my excuse for not calling? We had an understanding, but still. At least I'm not running from the phone this time.

"Hello ... " My voice barely cracks the surface.

"Jackson, I'm so glad to finally get you." Her voice brings me back to my other life, the one in Gravelsburg, with football parties, performance assessments, and responsibilities.

"I know how busy you get. Is everything all right? I mean with your dad and everything?" Her way of saying, it's okay you haven't called. My hand stops shaking.

"Fine." She knows how he is.

"I'm coming to visit. I'm driving my mom out to Fischer's Point tomorrow, not far from the lodge. I'll stop by. I haven't seen you in almost two weeks."

Of course, she is, she's had enough waiting. There's little I can do when Bri makes up her mind. We resolved our last argument, but resolve isn't enough. Going back to how we were before, that's what we're hoping for. I hardly remember what the last argument was about, but I'm sure it was my fault. Maybe her visit will cheer Artie up a little.

"I miss you, too," I whisper, real low. Feeling even more guilt, because I'm not sure if it's true. But it might make her feel better.

We say goodbye. Having her visit this den of wolves doesn't make me very comfortable. Rick will say something offensive. It's what he finds entertaining. But I should remember that Bri can hold herself against anyone, far as I've seen, and has never been fazed by Rick's lack of subtlety.

"So, you boys saw a black bear?" he asks.

"Um, yeah, east of the river." I swallow the bite in my mouth. "Down toward the creek. You know, where the peregrine's nest is." A prime example of a lie that keeps on growing. There is a massive-sized nest out at Teller's Ridge, a little closer from where Art and I almost lost our way. Been there since I can remember. Ever since we started coming out to the lodge. Since before Mom died.

"We should head out after eating," Rick says. "The bears are a little drunk from hibernation, shouldn't be too tough."

It's a little early for bear hunting, but the law isn't going to stop these guys. "No, shouldn't be."

"Why didn't you go for it?" Rick asks me.

"I didn't have my gun."

He knows Artie hates hunting. I only went along with it so Art and I could get away from the others. Not a good cover if you're hunting without a gun in tow. If we hung out with them, they'd try and get Artie to shoot something just to mess with him, and think it was funny.

But I've killed before.

My first, and only time, Rick was right there behind me, holding my hands to the rifle. He stood with his breath on my neck, his heart knocking against my head, and slowly he pressed his fingers on top of mine. When the rifle exploded I jumped back. He started laughing.

We shot the deer. He pulled me over to the animal lying in the grass; the blood flowed and pooled around its body. The buck lay there, still breathing, dying a slow death. It's one eye pierced straight through me. He stuck my hand in the hot blood and forced me to smear it across my face, saying, "For St. Hubert" the patron saint of hunters. It smelled of stale, metallic rain and animal dung. This was soon after Mom passed, and luckily for Artie, he was younger, maybe Rick felt he needed me, the older brother to be stronger and ready. Ready for what hasn't happened yet. He was always in a hurry to turn us into men.

Turning Artie and me into men became even more urgent for him after Mom's cancer took the last of her. By the time we found out, it had become very aggressive, and our once lively kitchen turned to darkness. Our family meals disappeared. The laughter disappeared; only shards of distant memories remain in that house. They told us she didn't have to suffer long, but I didn't believe it.

There was plenty of suffering, enough for her and our whole family. The depth of her pain I'll never know. Mom always had a smile on her face for me and for Artie. She was stronger than the three of us put together.

That was a long time ago, and it's been the three of us since then—no pets, Rick doesn't want them—no girlfriends; he doesn't want those, either. I've started to think he's punishing himself. You'd think after five years we could all move on. We haven't.

The grey of the afternoon reminds me of this stalemate: the unmoving sky, the stillness of the animals, the birds. The quiet isolated feeling of the lodge. The loneliness.

Just as the woodland creatures hide in their dens, protected from the icy drips of rain. We hide, but protected from what? Artie and I sleep in the den with our worst fear.

Gunner begins barking. Something's approaching the turkeys. I check out the window as Mr. Gallows walks over to see what's happening. The barks from the Shepherd intermix with growls, and then a whimper. His fur stands straight up. I don't see anything out back.

Mr. Gallows goes for his rifle. I turn around and there it is, the big black bear, about to make me honest. Awakened from its long hibernation and hungry, on the trail of blood and getting closer.

Mr. Gallows face is stiff with anticipation. He opens the back door. I thought the bear might see him, but it doesn't. With a mind set on a bellyful of wild turkey, dangling on the line just for him, the bear stays his course. The bear doesn't know yet, it's not going to be easy. Mr. Gallows holds steady in the doorway, rifle against his cheek, one eye closed. The bear is near the fence. Mr. Gallows' Shepherd stays at his heels, and won't stop barking. "Shh," he whispers to the dog. "Steady."

But nothing's about to stop that bear from getting those free-range turkeys. The bear passes the gate, thinking it's a glorious day.

"Arthur, what are you doing?" someone asks.

Artie starts throwing empty beer cans outside. It's obvious to me what he's doing.

"Are you crazy," Mr. Gallows whispers. "Rick, get your kid." He raises his voice. Standing in the doorway, stiff, one eye hidden in the viewfinder. "Artie, boy, you gotta stop."

Nothing's going to stop that bear -- except.

The shot rings out. Birds fly from the trees, and the bear drops to the ground, holding one dead turkey in its mitt. The Shepherd stays behind Mr. Gallows while he goes outside to inspect.

The massive bear lies in a pool of its own blood and turkey blood. I check in on Artie, his eyes fill with the tears he holds in.

The men gather around the bear, laughing and carrying on. One of them tries to lift the bear, but it's no use. Pete Winger and one of the new guys, act like the kids at my school, the ones you steer clear of, the ones who start trouble to entertain themselves because small minds need the suffering of others for entertainment.

The grown men buffoon around and lift the enormous leg and drop it a couple times. Are they making sure it's dead? I'm sure they feel powerful. Or maybe Mr. Gallows does since he shot it. Must weigh hundreds of pounds even after hibernation. It takes four of them to lift the animal, mostly by dragging it toward the "scraping house", which is what Artie and I call the shed because of the sounds we heard echoing out of there as kids.

Is this my future if I stay in Gravelsburg -- would I turn to such crude forms of entertainment? A fire swells, the anger Bri warned me about seeps up. I can taste it. I have to pull myself away from here.

If I think it's hard watching this spectacle, it's damn near ripping Artie's heart out. But Artie isn't watching. I turn back to the bear, defenseless and dead. The majestic animal gone in one shot, wasted. It leaves me with more emptiness, hollow, and removed from the world. But I can't walk away. I watch Rick reach over the bear, about to take the turkey from its grip -- the bear swipes him across the face. A howl of agony slices the air.

Three shots fire out.

Mr. Gallows finishes his work. Rick stands, holding his face, and when he removes his hand, three distinct mauled markings shine in crimson. He collapses onto the bench against the shed. One of the guys gives him a bandana. I can bet his drinking has numbed most of the pain.

"Should I call the doctor?" I ask, in a brief moment of pity seeing him crumpled over, weakened.

Rick yells at me to get out of there, and go and hide with Artie, wherever he is. Obviously not in enough pain if he has the strength to shout at me, trying to help.

I go inside to find my brother and hold down my own pain. Men don't cry. Right? Men are supposed to hide their emotions. That's the gospel according to our father, Mr. Rick Bower. Well, only tender emotions, anger is always encouraged. Bri was right.

Now I remember what our last argument was about.

"Hey, Artie. Want to go the duck pond?"

You can guess what he answers.

$$\maltese \quad 2 \quad \maltese$$

The sky doesn't change. No telling what time it is without a clear distinction of where the sun sits on the horizon. It could be morning; it could be twilight. Geese fly overhead, squawking the "almost dinner time" calls that tell us it's near sunset.

"When do you think we're going home?" Artie throws a stick into the pond.

"Soon, probably the day after tomorrow, or at least before school starts up again. I've got things to do."

"Like, see Brianna?" He breaks a long stick in half. "She misses you."

I try and remember the fun times, hear her laugh. She's laughing, and so is Artie. The leaves are all over the place. Artie and Brianna are chasing each other through the piles. I'm struggling to keep order and keep the piles together.

"Come on guys!" I shout at them.

Brianna picks up an armload of moldy leaves and throws them over my head. I'm annoyed, and then Artie does the same, blinding me with the debris.

"Can you stop? Be serious for once?"

"Serious? Is that what you want, Jackson?" she asks me.

Artie's still laughing and throwing leaves over her head. She reminds me of the Ophelia painting that hangs in Ludwig Hall, with twigs and leaves twisted through her hair, and she's giving me that same distant look. Waiting for me to come to my senses.

"Come on, Jackson!" Artie yells. Laughing so hard his face is flushed, and his cheeks are as red as the Macintosh apples lying on the ground. "I'll help clean up," he says. "Don't be so sore."

"Me, too," she says. "But I hope I at least get a kiss out of it."

"Look, I'm sorry." I take her hands and brush the crumpled leaves away. They're warm. Artie begins what he's promised, taking scoops of leaves and rearranging the piles. He looks up every few minutes to see if we're going to make up this time.

"You don't like us messing with your piles," she teases.

Her mouth drops slightly, strands of hair stick to her mouth, she looks so pretty with her cheeks flushed pink. I lift the strands away a few at a time, but instead of kissing her, which I should have done, I say, "No, I don't like doing things over, again and again, but so long as you and Artie are on the case."

"Always." She smiles. "You need to lighten up."

"Lighten up?" I pull her into my arms. She nods. I like seeing her covered with plants, and tree debris, like she's free, the way we used to be, carefree without adult issues. "I'm taking you to the clinic."

She falls into my chest, her breath is deep and she looks up. "Okay."

~

BEFORE I SAY ANYTHING, Artie asks, "You ever wonder how Mom and Dad ever fell in love?"

I didn't see that coming. I know he's been thinking about Mom a lot lately.

The damp breeze blows against us, brushing the curls off his face. He resembles her with his sleepy hazel eyes and freckles, and the sandy curls Rick tries to keep short, saying he looks like a girl if his hair isn't cut.

I look more like Rick, "stout, straight, and staunch" as Grandpa Bower likes to reiterate. "Us, Bower boys," he'll say, and knock me hard on the back. Artie usually gets: sensitive, sullen, and star struck—or dreamer. Rick calls him a dreamer as if it's the worst offense in the world. He's not only a dreamer he's the 200-meter Freestyle county champ at Marlington Pembrook High School. But it's not "man" enough for Rick. Wish I had the determination Artie has. Like becoming a vegetarian, against all odds, Artie's stance against the one person still in control of our lives. My god, it's a good thing he's so determined, 'cause it sure helps when your own family keeps knocking you down.

Faint chirps rise from the tall grass and become louder. Artie alerts me as he makes his way over to the originating direction. I follow him into the meadow. He crouches down and reaches into the grass.

"You can't pick up a baby bird, the mother will never want it."

"It's okay," he whispers.

A bird's nest in the grass, I'm surprised a carnivorous animal hasn't devoured it already. Suppose the wind blew it into the meadow, and there he goes, picking up the damn chick with his bare hands. Looks like a Robin, with its bulging eyes and orange beak.

"What are you gonna do with it?"

Artie cups the tiny bird in one hand, and squats into the grass; I watch him dig. He pulls up a worm and begins feeding the chick.

"This little fledgling is hungry." He holds the worm while the chick grabs it like spaghetti. "And it's not true about the moms deserting their babies after humans touch them. We'll fix the nest back in the tree, and its mom will find him again. Doesn't look injured. Eat up, little guy," he says to the bird.

I try and find anything I can use as a pulley, so I can help Artie return the nest. We comb through the soggy grass. He slips the wet bird into his jacket pocket. That should dry the fledgling.

He shouts that he's found something and brings it over. "Here's a willow branch. I thought it'd make a good cord, it's long and bendable."

I agree. We gather a few more willow branches and twist them together. The excessive rain has made them extra pliable. I follow Artie, making his way into the woods for the nearest tree.

"The nest had to blow from one of these." He hands me the nest after he slips in a layer of moss.

I take the willow branch, wrap the nest as secure as I can, and knot it to the tree. He hands me the chick wrapped in Kleenex. Artie always keeps tissues or a cotton bandana in his pocket for his frequent bloody noses. Another thing he and Mom share.

I lay the tiny wisp of a bird inside the nest, and before Artie says anything, I make sure to wrap more moss around the chick.

"Here, give him these." Artie drops three muddy wriggling worms in the center of my hand. I stretch up and place them inside.

"That should do it." I pat Artie's head. "Another job well done." He isn't impressed.

Darkness has crept in. We don't usually stray too far from the lodge, especially this late, and have only come out to Neumanville about a handful of times since Mom died. We know it somewhat, not as well as we should.

We'll have to cut through part of the woods to get back, at least to where the trillium flowers line the creek. We don't have anything with us, not even a flashlight, and it's at least a fifteen-minute hike.

The woods become dark. It's already wet. And just as we enter the umbrella of trees, the mist of rain turns into shower of ice water. The space between the trees allows the rain full access to us in steady pulses. We pull our windbreakers over our heads, trying to keep any small part of us dry, but of course, it's useless. In the pitch black, we press on. I follow Artie.

I follow him for over ten minutes, our heads half-hidden under jackets, and he stops. "Jackson, I can't see anything."

Neither can I, but we have to keep going. "Keep straight," I yell over the torrent of rain pounding my windbreaker. Nothing in the world could be darker than this moment. No direction. Not a hint of starlight.

Wet leaves spring back at me from Artie traipsing ahead. The branches sag; heavy from the constant spring rains, rain that could go on all night. I scrape against a large rock I might recognize from another trip; one daylight trip, but there're boulders everywhere. I reach out; a life raft, and cling to it. "Artie, hold on." My eyes focus. Something glints from the rock, maybe it's made of quartz; the only glimmer of light of any kind in over fifteen minutes. I'm not sure where the light's reflecting from unless it glows with its own luminescence. The rain continues its deluge, pouring buckets over us like a constant waterfall. Streams flow under our feet. We can expect flash floods.

"Stand under the boulders." I shout. My voice disappears under the downpour. We have reflectors on our windbreakers I can at least track his movements. "Until it lets up," I shout louder.

It's a slight overhang, a tiny lip, and we wait, standing under the boulder's protection. I press back against the rock, and the rain stops hitting my jacket like a timbale drum. I move closer to Artie and put my arm around him. He's shaking. I rub his shoulders in an attempt to warm him. I think about Rick Bower, sure he's passed out on the couch from all the drinking. I can bet he'll drink extra heavy tonight to numb the pain from the mauling.

Then it occurs to me if we get lost no one will come looking for us until the morning—not until late morning—tomorrow.

I can't see more than five feet ahead. Artie's quiet.

"Don't worry, Art, we'll be out of here soon."

"I know," is all he says.

I worry, even if Artie's used to standing strong. I think he makes himself believe he's not scared, just a little.

The rain seems to slow. I start to make out our surroundings, and when I'm sure the rain has let up, we walk away from the boulders.

The ground slopes; my feet don't recognize the descending path. Artie's a few paces ahead.

He screams.

I reach out, thinking I can catch him.

"Artie!"

I slide into a rapid descent. Unable to slow, I grab at the grass. I grab rocks. I have to keep up with him, and I let go. Artie's too far away, I don't see him.

The rains pound down.

❧   3   ❧

Thick mud. It's warm under the layers I've dug on my way down. But I'm not at the bottom. I've landed in a pine tree; the needles burrow unsympathetically under my jacket and into my skin.

"Art, where are you?" I hear nothing. "Artie!"

Darkness covers everything, except for a slip of sky filled with clouds. I catch a glimpse of the disappearing sunset.

"I'm okay, I think? I'm down here."

He doesn't sound too far. "Where, Artie, where?"

"I see you, I see your reflectors," he yells. "I'm right here!"

I dig my heels into the mud, and maneuvered my way toward him, following the sound of his voice. A white handkerchief waves in the air, there's barely enough light, but I can pinpoint his location.

"Are you okay?" I ask. "Shit, that was scary. Here, let me help you up." I take his hand.

"I can't move."

"Whadda you mean you can't move?"

"I'm stuck, my ankle -- hurts, bad."

I reach down, and feel for his leg, following to the end of his ankle. His legs are knee-deep in a hole between a rock and a pit, inside a trap made for a bear, I presume. It's a crude trap covered over with branches. Artie's not in the pit; he's managed to grab hold of enough branches and use them as a break. "How bad does it hurt?"

"Killing—it's really, really bad." His voice cracks, pushing each syllable out.

"Can you move it?"

"Probably, if it wasn't stuck. I can wiggle my toes."

I go behind him and pull, and pull. In-between, he moans in agony until I pry him loose. His ankle's twisted or something, and luckily not broken. I help Artie hobble the rest of the way down the ravine. We're very near the bottom already. Thankfully the rain stays back through the ordeal.

There's a clearing ahead of us, and light in the clouds. They must reflect some of the lights in Gravelsburg, twenty miles away, the largest city to Marlington Pembrook, our hometown, and home of the Pembrook Panthers.

"Where are we, Jackson?" He still doesn't sound too worried, but I sure am.

Fear is something I could always taste, like now. I sense it. I know when something bad is around the corner. Whether it's Rick yelling and lashing out. Or the fear of losing Mom, watching her die a little every day; knowing she was that much closer to leaving our lives, forever. Or leaving Artie behind for college to deal with our father alone. Fear of not making the grades because I want out, out of Marlington Penbrook, but certainly not this way. Not lost in the woods.

If a cell phone worked around here it would have been in my pocket. But the mountains make that impossible. I loop my arm around Artie's waist. "Don't worry, we'll figure something out."

I carry most of his weight. He's so light I could lift him, but he doesn't want me to. He prefers to hobble.

The rain returns in full force, falling harder than before. We need shelter, but where? I start thinking about the bears. Would they be out in the rain? Would one of them be angry about losing a mate earlier today?

I walk us forward, with no idea of where to go. Somehow, maybe it's my night vision kicking in, I make out the outline of a large stretch of pine trees up ahead. One's tall enough we can probably stand under them. I hold Artie as we crouch under its branches.

The giant pine shelters us from most of the deluge.

Our windbreakers are soaked, dripping with more rain than passes under the tree. I take a couple of sticks, and fasten our jackets into a canopy, weaving them into a low-hanging branch. The ground is too wet to sit on, so we squat, and wait.

"My ankle—hurts, so bad, Jackson, like it's on fire." He squeezes my arm, holding his balance.

"You can still wiggle your toes, right?"

"Yeah..." Artie needs to get the weight off his foot. I take his jacket from the branch and lay it on the ground, a thin layer of protection from the pine needles and damp earth.

"Sit here and rest your foot."

I feel Artie's leg to get an understanding of how bad it is. Sure wish I had my flashlight. His leg is completely soaked, as can be expected. I feel his ankle, and he muffles more groans. It could be covered in blood for all I know.

"How bad is it, now?"

"Real bad. I think it's cut pretty deep."

"You have that handkerchief?"

He hands it to me.

"I can't see a thing. Can you wrap it and I'll help tie it on."

Artie rumples around and elbows me, and I finished the job.

"Is that any better?" I ask.

"A little."

What does it matter now? We're drenched to our bones. I keep my windbreaker in the branches, falsely imagining it'll dry under the pine tree. Artie's on top of his, and thankfully he gets some relief from tying up his ankle. I lean against the tree; rainwater trickles down its truck and onto my back. It's cold. Artie's teeth won't stop chattering. I try and warm him as much as I can. Thoughts of hypothermia, and shock, and what if we die here compete for my attention. What if Artie dies? What's wrong with me?

I erase the thoughts from my head and replace them with the variety of trees found in the North Woods. I mentally list them: Red Adler, hemlock, pine, maple, mulberry, oak, beech, it keeps my head busy, clears the fear sticking to my tongue.

I wrap myself over Artie's torso, while he reclines on my lap, and I hold him tight. The way I held Brianna. Before. She's going to be in Pine Ridge tomorrow, and I won't be there.

Artie and I cling to each other's warmth; he steadies my shaking. If he doesn't get hypothermia it'll be a miracle. We have to make it to the morning.

In the morning there'll be light.

"I'll stay up and keep you warm," I tell him. "I won't let you go." It's what I said to Brianna.

I park the green Honda.

"It's okay if you drive," she says. "I'm not in the mood anyway."

I turn to her and wait.

"If you want to take Beatrice Road, go ahead. Either way will get us there."

"But, you wanted to stop for ice cream?"

"I lost my taste for it now. Soon this will all be over. I can't wait." She blows her hair out her face and crosses her arms.

How can she give up like that? What if she doesn't know what she's doing — what if she thinks she's making the right decision and changes her mind about that too? It'll be too late. She can't decide what she wants to eat, or road to take — and just wants it to all be over. Gone. Like it never happened.

"You're doing it again."

"What?"

"Ignoring me."

"No, I'm not," I tell her. " I'm doing exactly what you said, taking East Essex.

"And giving me the silent treatment — like you-know-who."

She knows I hate being compared to him. As if I were like him. I don't leave the people I care about. Or become an emotional rock.

I screeched off the road's shoulder and entered Essex road, and continued to Whitmaker's homemade ice cream. I'd have an ice cream, even if she'd changed her mind.

＃ 4 ＃

Something kicks me. "Stop it, Artie." I moan, thinking I'm in the bottom bunk at home.

Again, a hammer falls onto my foot.

"Jackson, wake up." Artie's voice hovers above my head. Who's kicking my foot? I spring up, alarmed.

Standing over us is what I think was once a man, hunched over, his face hidden beneath a year's growth of facial fur; his hair in dreadlocks, if they're intentional. He looks disgruntled, and maybe a little pissed off. He's enormous from my view, almost as tall as the tree that half-covered us through the night.

The man holds a tall stick and he keeps knocking my foot with it. I retract my leg. Then he points the stick at Artie's foot and doesn't say anything. My eyes follow his direction.

The handkerchief and the bottom of Artie's pants are covered in blood. I think about predators, and realize how lucky we are none came for us last night. It must have been the rain keeping them away. "Artie—your foot!"

"It's OK, doesn't hurt too much right now."

The grizzly man towering over us uses his walking stick as a pointer. He points at Artie's foot and then he points in the direction he expects us to follow, like some deranged mime. "I'm Jackson Bower, and this is my brother, Arthur. Do you have a telephone we could use?"

He says nothing, and shakes his head, or is it a nod?

It's hard to tell. Could have been a shiver. He makes the motion for us to follow him, swaying that stick of his forward. I hoist Artie up against my shoulder and march ahead.

We come out of the clump of dense trees. I glance up. It's a relief the rain has stopped. I recognize the steep ravine we traveled down last night.

It's over 100 feet, or 30 meters high, about the size of a ten-story building. Steep and covered over with bare branches, that could have easily impaled us. I count our good fortune and silently give thanks.

The old man stays in the lead, leaving a rank trail behind him; a mixture of skunk and rotted fruit from a garbage pail. I make sure to shift myself, and Artie, out of his downwind. He moves slow, in part because we are. Also, because he's dragging his left foot along while leaning on the support of his walking stick.

We follow him over rocks and brambles and arrive at another crude trap similar to the one Artie got caught in. The old man fixes a few things on the trap. Finishes and points the stick ahead. What choice do I have?

I have no idea where we are. Artie can barely walk and he's in excruciating pain. He keeps biting his lip. He screams out and muffles it right away. It's the first time the old man stops. He turns around and looks at us. Then walks on.

We pass over a stream and follow it for a while.

It's very early in the morning. I imagine Rick Bower's searching for us with the entire police department by now.

It's getting harder to hold on to Artie and not slip on the rocks. I make measurements of my surroundings, marking territory in the endless trees, barely decipherable from the next. Red

Oak and hemlock, pine trees, I try and pinpoint anything distinguishable.

The sun edges above the horizon of pine trees in the east. I have some bearing of our direction. We're walking south. I check the clouds; it doesn't look like any immediate threat of rain. The old man waves his stick to the right and we followed right.

Eventually, we come to a small clearing. Deer skulls and a mix of rodent bones lay around a pit once used for fire. It's burnt black and washed out. The pit sits near the opening of a cave of a massive boulder, a few meters away. He motions for us to sit among the bones of squirrel and deer heads. I inspect them closely for human bones.

We sit down. Artie's relieved to get off his one good foot. "I think he's trying to help us," he whispers.

I'm not convinced. I looked over my shoulder. The old man disappears into one of the boulders that must be the mouth of a cave.

My windbreaker's almost dry, but the rest of my clothes are wet. The clinging cold digs into me. I imagine Artie feels much worse, cold and wet, with his foot going from numbness to being on fire. "Let me see." I wonder how bad it is, in case we need to take off running.

Artie grimaces and flexes his leg toward me. I unwrap the handkerchief. His foot swells behind purple bruising, and there're deep gashes around his ankle. I wish we'd kept our hiking boots on. It isn't broken and it doesn't appear he'll bleed to death. Not anymore. He just needs some cleaning up and antibiotics.

The old man returns to us. With light now on his face I see he isn't that old. His hair is kind of grey, part dirty-blonde, and full of rat-tails, which is what Mom called giant knots. I'm sure he hasn't seen a comb in years. He doesn't have his walking stick and comes at us slow and steady, dragging his foot, and he's holding something in a basket.

He sits down on a rock.

Our host motions for Artie to pass his foot over. After Artie does, he peels off the handkerchief and tosses it into the pit of bones. He rips the pants from the bottom, already torn, and takes a brown glass bottle and pours whatever's inside all over Artie's ankle. I expect Artie to scream out. He only squints. Artie's been in so much pain already, I imagine the bottle's contents have little bearing. The old man takes a swig from it. He reaches into his basket and pulls out a white sterile bandage from a sealed plastic bag. I stare at the contrast of the white bandage against his burnt brown, mud, encrusted fingernails. In what seems like a second thought, he pulls out a tube of ointment. There's no label.

"Is that antibiotic?" I ask.

He glances at me, like what else would it be? He squeezes some of the contents onto the gauze, and lays it gently across Artie's open wound, as if he knows exactly what he's doing, and wraps his ankle.

"Do you have a phone?

He shakes his head. At least he can hear me.

"We have to find our way back to Eagle's Stone Ridge. Do you know the way?"

He stays focused on wrapping Artie's foot. After a few minutes, he abruptly points behind him. Behind him is the cave.

"I'm sorry, sir, and I want to thank you for helping my brother with his foot, but we're lost. We need to find our way back."

The old man doesn't speak. I decide he's mute. He replaces everything inside the basket and takes it with him into the cave.

I turn to Artie. Artie shrugs.

"He's got to know his way around," I tell Artie. "He's probably been living in the woods for years." Judging from the smell.

The sun has climbed to the peak of the trees, moving us into the early afternoon.

"You think Dad's worried?" he asks.

"He'll be out looking for us, don't worry about that," I say, half-convincingly.

"Sure am hungry. I haven't eaten anything since that pickle tomato sandwich, yesterday."

I nod, agreeing that we need food.

Brambles surround us. I know of a few things we can eat in the forest, but I don't see any. There are pine trees. Although it's not the season for harvesting the nuts, we could chew the pine needles for energy if needed.

He's back. His hands are full, holding a large pot. He sets it down and pulls a few items from it, placing them on a wood plank he's wiped with the back of his hand: Three potatoes, one whole white cabbage, grass clippings—or are they wild chives? He drops a few small bones; most likely chicken bones and wanders off again into the cave.

"Looks like lunch." Artie quips, sounding slightly more comfortable at this point.

Before long, the man returns, and he's carrying four liter-sized brown bottles in a wire bin. The bottles are the same size as the one he poured over Artie's foot. He leaves the bottles on the side.

"I understand you can't talk, but you can hear me, right?" I ask.

He looks up from counting supplies. He's disgruntled as if I continuously interrupt his train of thought. His only response is to pull a large chopping knife from the bottom of the pot and begin chopping the grass clippings on the board like a professional chef. This man has a past.

Making a gesture that he's forgotten something, he stops, stands up, and searches through his stuff.

"I hope we're not lunch," Artie whispers.

I've started to wonder myself.

The old man smiles, suddenly, and it's not a lightly humored kind of smile, more like a kid on Christmas morning smile, a deranged kid. He starts laughing.

This does not convince me his plans aren't to have us for his lunch. His unexpected excitement gives me the impression he's a little out of his head, for sure. His laugh is clown-like and painted, appearing almost painful with the creases carving into his face. Reminding me of Rick.

He leaves for the cave, once again.

I remember a time when our father laughed, a real kind of laugh, and a memory that hasn't completely disappeared.

A string of multi-colored bulbs are the only lights on when he comes home, soaking wet, and smiling. Mom takes his coat as he shakes the sleet from his hair.

"You got it?" she whispers.

"I did," he says, patting the bag, and reaches in to pull out two silver wrapped packages. "A five-hour line couldn't stop me. The boys are going to be so surprised."

"Shh," she giggles. "You did good." Mom kisses him, and when she looks up the stairs she sees me sitting there. "Now you go to bed, Jackson, nothing going on down here."

"Dad, are those the Special Edition Chrono-Raiders? You got them?" I wanted to shout it but didn't want to wake Artie up and spoil the surprise.

"Honestly, I don't know what you're talking about." Mom smiles.

He runs up the stairs, scoops me up, and throws me over his shoulder, and marches me right back into bed. Tucking the blankets around me, he says I have to wait the three more days till Christmas, just like everybody else.

I couldn't believe he waited in line all day, something none of the other dads would do. He'd made the time. I was happy and knew Artie would be even happier because the Chrono-Raiders were the one thing he wanted for Christmas. He'd even asked to make it a combo present for his birthday, months away.

THIS TIME, the man is back, with a grill lighter and burlap sack. He dumps the sack of coal into the pit.

I look up at the grey clouds about to cover the sky, expecting rain any minute. He stuffs newspaper into the pit. I wonder how and where he bought the newspaper. I want to see the date on that paper. Before my thoughts and actions meet up, he has it on fire, delighted with watching the flames ignite the charcoal until a ring of fire wraps the iron pot.

Artie and I watch each other through the flames as he pours all four bottles' contents inside the pot, and resumes chopping the herbs and cabbage. When he finishes he adds them into the pot. He adds the presumed chicken bones. I really want to believe they're chicken bones. He's saved one and chews it while stirring the pot. If he's not cooking us I wonder if he plans on sharing? It's not as if we have a two-way conversation going on.

Artie and I are hungry and tired and weak. If we don't come down with something awful after sleeping in the rain all night it would be miraculous.

The man looks up from his work and smiles again. "I'll be right back." He speaks! The man can talk. But the words sound like another language. Grabbing the basket, he limps over to the brambles about 20 feet away and begins picking in the weeds. He tosses whatever he's found inside the basket and returns to us.

Inside the basket are tiny wild strawberries, mostly white. He seems pleased. With his crumpled, oversized mitt, he hands a few berries to Artie. Artie scoops them up and tosses them into his mouth. He gets a kick out of watching Artie gobble up the berries, and offers him more from his tar-stained hands.

I pass. Guess I'm not as hungry as Artie is. Knowing where they came from, I figure I might pick some later on my own.

He stirs the pot. You know, it begins to smell pretty good, and the bones do smell like chicken. Wonder if Artie's going to mind chicken parts in his soup today? The man reaches for a ladle and scoops deep into the pot. He brings it up and takes a long breath. Appears, he likes the smell. With his lips puckering up like a fish; he slurps the hot soup from its edge, and he's not quiet about it.

He looks at me then at Artie. Lays the ladle on the side of the pot, and disappears into his cave. Again. I want to follow him this time. Does he really live there, or is he camping out?

"What do you think's in that cave?" I whisper to Artie.

He's playing with a soldier beetle that's landed on his knee, and shrugs.

"We have to get back." I keep my voice low.

"You think he has a cell phone in there?" he asks.

"If he does, it won't work. There isn't a cell tower for miles."

The old man stands over us. Holding a tray with bowls and what I'm sure is bread. My mouth salivates. He squats over the fire and tosses the bread loaf on top of the coals. Oblivious to the heat, he reaches into the flame and turns it a few times. His fingers must have three inches of calluses. When he's sure the bread's hot enough, he throws it on the tray with the bread knife. With hands as dark as the bread he's burned, he reaches for a bowl and fills it. Then hands it to me.

Artie lingers over his new beetle friend. We both watch him, but Artie doesn't pay attention to us. Our host begins to slice the bread, but more or less breaks it off and hands me a piece. "You care about small creatures, huh?" he asks Artie. "My son cared for animals. He cared for all the gentle creatures."

Artie turns to him and smiles easily. "Does he live here, too?"

"Thanks." I take the bread, watching his response but he doesn't answer, just stares into the fire.

The soup smells good and I'm beyond starving. The grass clippings *are* wild chives. Reminding me of Mom's soups and her chili, even her tuna casserole. What I wouldn't give for a slice of her tuna casserole right now, though I always hated it.

"Smells good," Artie says.

The old man snaps out of his thoughts and hands Artie a bowl.

"There're chicken bones in it..." I tell him.

"I know." He sets the beetle on his shoulder, leans over with the bowl, and waits for his serving. The old man fills it to the rim. Artie sips thoughtfully, while the beetle crawls along his arm.

I finish my soup and the two small potatoes at the bottom,

chewing them quickly to get to my question. "Did you have an accident?" I ask, referring to the leg he drags.

Without pulling the bowl from his mouth, he gives me a look that's neither threatening nor amicable, more like he didn't understand what I said. His grey and furry eyebrows close in tight and he resumes drinking his soup until the last gulp. Then clears his throat. "No."

Thinking there's an explanation to come, I wait, but he reaches for more scorched bread. Breaks a few pieces and drops them on the tray. He gnaws on the rest as he stands up and limps toward the cave.

"Guess, you upset him," Artie says.

"Yeah, maybe, but man, Artie, we've gotta get home."

Artie doesn't seem as anxious as I am.

When our host returns this time, it's with a large hardcover book. He lowers it carefully onto the rock between us, as if it's made of glass, and sits down.

It's a photography book, a photography book with scenes from the Iraq War. The old man freezes, holding it in his lap.

"Is this something you want to show us?" I ask.

He turns and watches Artie for several minutes too long as if looking at something he never wants to forget. Maybe he didn't hear me. I reach out for the book; he yanks it closer to him. He tries to say something, but he starts crying. Or I think he is. Hunched over the book, his entire body begins to heave and he's sobbing like a baby. I check in with Artie to mark his expression. He's as confused as I am. The man wipes the tears from the cover with his coat sleeve while trying to calm down.

Artie gets up and puts his hand on his shoulder. "It's okay, mister. It's all over now." I didn't think it was the best thing to say, considering he now lives in a cave.

He sucks in a long breath. "They took my son. He sputters, shaking as he speaks, rocking his body back and forth. "My only son. At the beginning of his life." His voice breaks into pieces. Possibly, the most words out of him in weeks, maybe years?

Then I realize his son must have been in the Iraq War.

"There's a photo of my beautiful boy here, in this book," he says, gulping air in-between gasps of pain. Cries, like none I've ever heard from a grown man. I never hear Rick cry. I don't know if he's ever cried over Mom. I can't remember, but then again, Rick Bower wasn't there when she died.

He left me alone with Artie. Grandpa Bower came hours later, hours after the nurses had to calm our hysteria, hours after the agony of holding Artie. He cried so hard, for so long, until he stopped crying, and stopped talking. I haven't heard Artie cry since.

The old man swipes more tears with his sleeve. "There's a photo of Anatole in this book," he says, drying a hand on his patched-up overcoat. Artie stands over him, patting and rubbing his shoulders, whispering to him, the way he comforts a wounded animal.

"You look much like my son when he was your age. He played with bugs, too, even cared for the neighbor's pets at home." He sniffs.

The old man reaches under his coat and pulls out a blue bandana and blows his nose. He seems to gain some composure. Then he wipes the book's cover with it and opens to the first page.

He turns another, carefully scanning each image. "He was only eighteen years old, a baby." It's as if he held his emotions back for years, until this moment, until the two boys he found in the woods brought him back to reality, somehow.

He stops turning the pages. "For what? FOR WHAT!" His voice roars above the treetops. Birds scatter. It's the first I hear the anger he's capable of. Artie looks down at me and I scoot in for a better look. There are five guys and a girl in the photo. All dressed in desert khakis, guns slung to their side, smiling and young, and not much older than me.

"I never saw him again. He was killed by 'negligent discharge' that's how they cover up the blow of what it really is—killed by his own people—fratricide. Anatole didn't want to be a killer; he wanted to come home." He turns to me. Waves of black soot roll over his face and drip like last night's rain to the ground.

"They were all killed. All five of them, not hours after this photo was taken." He mumbles something under his breath, but the words disappear.

Then he says, clearly, "I know how the military does things, hiding all evidence." He snaps the book shut. "Rain is coming."

All of his wailing stops with the snap of the book and he takes it with him into the cave. I watch him traipse away.

The sky grows dark. I check in with Artie, he nods.

I stand up and follow a few paces behind him into the mouth of the cave. He has to be completely out of his mind, and here I am, possibly heading right into a trap.

❧ 6 ❧

The cave is much larger than it appears from outside, must be carved into the side of the cliff. I move slow, careful not to get too close, but I know he hears my steps behind him.

Deeper in the cave, a small lantern burns. There's dampness and a dank odor that grabs my attention, and it mixes with the same putrid rotting fruit I smelled on the old man earlier. Water trickles down the wall of rock, landing into a puddle. The old man lights another lantern. He turns to me in a deliberate, aggressive manner, and says, "Watch your step."

I can't see much and decide it's best to stay put until I get a signal from him. In the dim light, I watch as he reaches for another lamp and lights it. The cave takes on an eerie glow. I sense Artie behind me.

Artie stands at the opening of the cave, waiting. The rain is falling hard behind him. It rings through the cave like a song of doom. Lighting the rest of the lanterns the old man expands the size of the cave, and I can see he's lived here for a very long time.

There are rows of shelves, stacked and filled with books, an architect's drafting table covered in papers, rulers, and T-squares, a desk with reference books left open. Off to one side is a makeshift kitchen. Hoses climb through buckets, and up along the stone, ending somewhere outside the cave. I imagine there's a bathroom hidden somewhere too.

"How long have you lived here?" I ask.

He places the lamp in the center of the desk and looks around before answering as if the answer floated somewhere in the air. "Ten years. Maybe?" He sniffs.

"Are you hiding from the police?" I didn't hear that question coming, but there it is. I wait, expecting him to say, yes, I'm hiding from the police, and I'm going to kill you and your brother, and eat the remains. I don't say it out loud, but at least I thought what I was afraid to think. Although at this point I kind of start feeling sorry for him. He doesn't answer my question, so I give him another to answer.

"So, what's your name?"

But again, he has better things to do than answer me and searches through papers on the desk. He looks up, eventually, somewhat surprised. "Gunther. Gunther Antwerp." I suppose he hasn't heard those two words in a while.

Gunther moves to the drafting table. Artie's hobbled over and stands across from him. I join them just as Gunther rolls up large pages from the drafting table and slips them out of sight.

"What are those drawings for?" I ask.

He doesn't answer. Instead, he pulls up the hood of his coat, grumbles a few words, and walks with one of the lanterns into the rain. He's very much like a bear, grunting and groaning, on his way out of the cave.

Wouldn't be evening yet, but with the grey world outside it's hard to tell it's only about lunchtime. Rick has to be worried by now. He'll come looking for us. Or will he abandon us as he did before? When we needed him?

Most likely, he's asleep, and on pain medication. He'll have no idea we're gone. No idea that Artie and I are lost in the woods with some wacko hermit on the other side of the ravine.

I walk to the mouth of the cave and stand there, watching the rain. I don't see the old man anywhere. "Will this rain ever stop? How are we going to get home?"

"We can't be too far," Artie says. "When the rain stops Dad'll come looking for us with the guys and the dogs, and they'll pick up our scent."

He sounds pretty sure.

"That man's got to know the way to East Point," Artie says. "Look at all his books. He knows a thing or two. You think he's read every one of them?" Artie sits down at the desk across from the drafting table.

"Probably, not much else to do around here," I say. "If he's lived in this cave and in the woods for ten years—he knows his way around. He was making traps like the one you fell in. Unless he plans on keeping us here."

The thought hangs on me like a noose, tightening its grip.

"Jackson, those drawings he hid—wait. Is he coming?"

I turn and look. "No."

"Get them out." Artie points to where the old man slipped them out of sight. "Hurry," he whispers.

I pull out the drawings and unrolled them across the table.

The top drawing is very technical and bears the stamp: USAF Air Ordinance Museum, Ft. Walton, Florida. Artie holds the lantern closer.

When my eyes adjust I notice it's a design for a rocket. The second sheet has sketches for some type of manmade bomb and lists supplies needed to build it.

"A bomb?" I stand there, unable to believe my eyes. "For what? What's he gonna blow up?"

The old man's on his way back. I can feel it. I roll up the draw-ings and stuff them back behind the boxes, and hurry over to stand at the entrance, with barely a moment spared; his lantern comes bouncing along in the fog. "He's coming back."

He's hunched over, carrying something massive over his shoulders. The lantern knocks from his belt strap. I turn to Artie. He's taken a book from a stack and pretends to read.

"Looks like he's got a something with him, something big."

Artie barely looks up and keeps reading.

He pushes through the cave opening. I move to the side. Heat rising from the deer waves inches from me. "Help me, would you," he orders, pressed down with the weight of the carcass.

I lift the deer; hot against my hands and body and heave it up along with him, until we're able to walk the deer to the hook in the corner.

"Hold steady."

I do as I'm told, and help him secure it to the hook. With a better view of the animal swinging in front of me, I can tell it's young. Artie isn't going to have any of this. Or would he?

"Couldn't find any rabbits in this rain, but, hell, venison's better." He wipes his hands on his coat. "A man cannot sustain by bone soup alone."

Tossing the "dreadlocks" behind his neck he takes a nearby rag and blows his nose into it like a trumpet. When he's completely finished clearing every last drop of snot, he sticks the rag into his back pocket. "Hold on," he says and walks away.

He takes an oil lamp raises it, and peers in my direction. "You can let go of that thing." Then he turns around and digs into a milk crate; clamoring through utensils, and pulls out a few kitchen tools. After a heavy once over through an assortment of blades he finds one he seems satisfied with, and comes toward me, glancing over his shoulder at Artie, who's very much engrossed in whatever book he's reading.

"That's a classic you got there, son. My favorite is Thoreau's essay *On The Duty of Civil Disobedience*. Read it a hundred times. Page 222.

Artie looks up and nods.

The old man takes hold of the deer. "Okay Jackson, steady, right there. '...When the government machine is producing injustice, it is the duty of conscientious citizens to be a counter friction— a resistance— to stop the machine' –hold steady, Jack. Steady."

With the short curved knife, he cuts into the end of the deer, hanging upside down, and continues slicing until the knife reaches its neck at the bottom. Then he separates the divide, exposing the entrails.

"Um." I stall, but it needs to be said. "It was really nice of you to help us out and all, but we have to get home. We could use your help finding the way back through the woods to East Point. Our father's lodge is there, past Teller's Ridge." He doesn't say anything, just keeps dragging the blade into the doe. The entrails drop into the bucket.

"Where are they? Shouldn't there be a search party out for you boys?"

He speaks the truth. Rick should be out with the guys and that damn Shepard looking for us. "He's probably still asleep. Or maybe they've started out by now?"

"You're letting it slip, don't let go," he orders.

I hold the warm fur, digging my fingers into the thick skin, gripping hard against the tug from its opposite side. Rips amplify throughout the cave as he separates the skin from the meat.

I want to let go. The smell of the flesh, raw and gamey, is an acrid smell, a sad smell. I have no stomach for this. I need to figure out how to get us out here, and back to the lodge. Bet he has no plans on helping us find our way to East Point.

With the rain constantly falling, and dark clouds covering any sense of light, it's impossible to know what time it is. Brianna must be at East Point by now. I have to stay aware of the time. I have to be ready. "What time is it?" I ask the old man. "Do you even have a watch?"

"Do I *even* have a watch? What tone of speaking is that?"

He's dead serious. His eyes corner mine. Evidently, he can switch at any minute. Even decide to kill us.

"I -- I'm sorry, sir. I didn't mean any disrespect, just wondered if you had any need for one." I hope he believes that.

Artie's watching us.

"No," he answers and goes back to his work. Concentrating, cutting deeper than before, and one by one, he pulls deer parts out and places them next to him on the metal tray. I'm thinking we aren't going to hear another word from him.

"It's near two o'clock," he says, surprising me. Wonder how he knows? Guess if you've lived deep in the woods, in a cave for years, you have a sixth sense about what time of day it is.

"You must know your way around the woods pretty good." I hold the carcass steady as if my life depends on it.

"...Very well."

"Do you know our lodge, over at East Point? On Eagle's Stone Ridge?"

"By the crow boulder and Tellers Ridge?" he says. "I know it, but we aren't traipsing around until this rain lets up. The flooding over the lake will make it impassible north of here. That's the trail you want. You both came over the ridge. Your brother, there." He slings the blade in Artie's direction. "Got caught in my bear trap. Good you didn't fall in." He shakes his head. "It'd've been worse than some fancy gash in your ankle. Hold still," he directs me. "You'd've drowned in that trap with the flash flooding."

It's hard to hold still with him yanking against me.

"When this rain stops I'm gonna start a fire again, and cook this up something special. You'll both be here for dinner by the looks of things."

He finishes tearing out the guts. Blood pours like the rain into the bucket drum. The old man pauses, wipes his bloody hands on the snotty rag then rubs his hands together. He appears to be in pain.

"My arthritis," he mutters. He removes the tray with entrails from my sight and sets them on a drying rack near the cave opening.

I let go of the carcass.

"I'll be back to finish skinning it." He gathers a few items into his jacket pocket and leaves.

I rub my hands from the cold. They're streaked with blood. The deer carcass swings, back and forth.

I start thinking being a vegetarian might be a good idea, except that I'm getting real hungry. I walk away from the carcass and toward the cave opening. He won't be gone long. Without wasting a second, I go to the back of the cave and search around.

Thunder rings out; Artie jumps.

Sure, there are books; lots of books, shelves and stacks, piled two feet high with books. They're everywhere. A man's gotta have entertainment. Artie manages to keep himself busy with a pile he's moved closer to him on the desk. I give him a look that's sure to question what he's up to.

"Well, we could be here a while," he says, sounding almost drunk, and resumes reading.

I roll my eyes. There has to be something, maybe a radio, around here? I scour the shelves, turning up dust, and hidden behind paper cups, I find a radio.

It works. Figures, the old man wouldn't leave himself out here without any way of knowing what's going on in the world. But the light on the radio flickers, maybe it's damp? Reception comes in and goes out. I switch to AM radio. The local news sputters out a weather report, confirming what the old man said. *There will be no relief from the rain today. More thunderstorms expected.*

If Rick sends out search parties, will the dogs pick up our scent? They probably won't in a downpour. I'm not feeling very good about any of this. But Artie seems fine. He's reading with a smile on his face.

The old man has to show us the way back. There's just too much rain right now. I leave the radio on. Elevator music mixes with static. A song Brianna loves plays over the airwaves. I don't know the name of it. She loves a lot of songs. Brianna will know I'm gone when she gets to the lodge. She'll wake Rick out of his dead zone.

I quickly unroll Gunther's drawings and try to read the writing under the lamp. There's a list of chemicals.

As I read my hands shake, making it almost impossible to understand. I can't hold the lamp steady. He plans to set a bomb off at The Worthington Center. The Worthington Center houses The State Civil Court and Sheriff's office of Warren County— that's ten miles from here. I almost drop the lamp.

"Artie." I ruffle through the drafting pages, wanting to read more, unable to believe my eyes. "He's planning to set off explosives at the Sheriff's office next to the Civil Court!"

Artie lifts the lamp over the drawings. I keep searching through the papers, where designs for small bombs and large bombs are not so well hidden. Artie looks up at me but doesn't say anything. He's captivated, scanning each sketch as if taking a snapshot photo to keep in his memory.

"The Shop and Save is there too. People go to the Worthington Center all the time. Innocent people," I say, making sure he hears me.

And for the first time, in a long time, I sense fear in Artie. But it's not for him, and it sure isn't for us. He fears for the people who'll be killed.

"It'll never happen," he finally says, as vague as if he were in a dream, and goes back to reading. He isn't acting like himself. Yes, he likes reading, about as much as I do, but Artie's in another place. I begin to feel alone and realize I have to make the plans to get us out of here.

I rush to roll up the drawings and knock the lamp, spilling the oil all over them. That's it. He'll know for sure we're on to him. I finish, hoping he doesn't examine the drawings before we're out of sight.

How can Artie be so optimistic? I suppose he gets that from Mom, too. But it's naïve, and could get a lot of people killed, including us. He must be delirious from the pain.

Then it hits me: the only shopping center for twenty miles is at the Worthington Center. If Brianna's at the lodge and needs food, she'll have to go there. Hell, you can't drink the water at the lodge. She'll have to buy water at that Shop & Save.

We have to get out of here.

The old man's cracked after so much time away from people, and there's no telling what he plans for us. He wants to set a bomb off in a government building that's attached to a shopping plaza. Those people just work there. They aren't responsible for his son's death. All I can think of is getting home. I walk over to see what's holding Artie's attention.

"What are you reading?"

He lifts the Thoreau book.

"If we can stop him he won't," Artie says.

"Stop what?" The old man's voice surrounds us.

"Stop you from going to all this trouble to make dinner for us," I answer. "You don't have to."

"Well, I gotta eat anyway." He pushes through with an armload of stuff and proceeds to the hanging slab of meat. "I'm gonna let this cool before slicing it. But the innards are good. We can cook those up real soon. Don't know about this rain, though. I'll have to make a fire at the opening so the smoke can escape." He pauses and slowly turns his head toward me, then Artie, and he looks at the desk. "You have the radio on?"

A weight hits my chest. The same feeling I get when someone wants to challenge me to a fight.

I clear my throat. "Um, thought there'd be a weather report."

"What'd they say?"

"Same as you. Rain all day and flash flooding."

"I have some dry stones. Here, will you help me out, Jackson."

I scramble over to him.

"Gather up stones that look like this." He lifts a smooth oval stone. Rocks line the front of the cave. "We'll make a circle," he says. "Got some dry wood in the corner. Shouldn't get too smoky."

"Artie, you wanna help?" I ask, wondering if his foot's any better, or if he can even walk after sitting so long.

"Leave the boy be, he's reading. Gotta make some sense of this world."

I know who the lackey is. I gather round stones and dry wood he has from a bin; make a circle, and toss the wood splints and chips into the center.

"All right. Good. You did good. Now, let's see, where'd I leave that grill rack?"

He moves to the boxes near the right of the cave's opening. I barely see him in the dark, but after a sweeping reach inside one of the boxes, he yells, "Ah, here."

"Haven't used the grill in a while?" I ask, finding it hard to believe.

"Just the soup pot." He shrugs. "Winter wasn't very kind, but with the spring, mealtime should be much more appetizing."

Springtime? He wants to keep us here?

I watch the carcass hanging in the corner; appetizing is not the word for it.

"You're getting a good education there, boy." Referring to Artie. "You're gonna need more oil in that lamp soon. It'll ruin your eyes with no light. Mine are going."

He leaves me with the grill to secure over the stones and then wanders over to a panel of shelves. "And you like to read, I better find the oil."

Artie turns when he realized he's being spoken to. His face sags from the tug of his hand used to prop his head.

The old man pulls down a milk crate. "Here, let's make sure

you keep your eyesight." He pours oil into the lamp and replaces the glass top.

"Much better. Thanks."

"Good. Good." He tousles Artie's hair. "My son loved reading. In fact, many of these books were his."

The room becomes significantly brighter as he fills two more lamps. Then he douses the pile of wood chips with the oil. "Just gotta light it."

I stand back. He reaches into his pocket and pulls out a box of matches, fumbling through them with his tarred fingers, and drops a few on the ground. "Eh, that's okay, they're waterproof." When he manages to pick one, he strikes it against the box, bends over, and ignites the pile of wood chips. "Damn arthritis."

I walk over to the fire. He's right, not too much smoke. Or at least most of it escapes the cave. I imagine leaving on that waft of smoke out of here and beg for a clearing.

The rain stops. It's stopped raining.

A patchwork of grey still fills the sky, but it looks promising. I take a few steps out, and hesitate, expecting a yank back inside the cave. Maybe, because the old man has collateral he allows me a few paces outside.

I turn to see what Artie thinks. He sits, reticent. I wouldn't be going far—not yet. Gunther can be sure of that.

I want to believe it's the rain that's kept the old man from taking us over the mountain. Who wouldn't be suspicious? The man's got plans. Secret, destructive plans, not one to be trusted by any means.

The ground sinks with my step. Its vise grip turns my sneakers into Frankenstein shoes with layers of mud. It feels good getting out of that cave. I feel lighter. How many hours have passed since this morning, since last night? Feels like we've been in there for over a week.

The woods stand silent ahead of me. The sulfuric odor of the entrails barely disguised within the wild onions blow past. A blue jay calls out for one of its own. Birds keep track of their family and have tight-nit groups. They take care of each other. Come on Rick Bower, come out and find your boys.

I feel warmth behind me.

"What are you out looking for, son?" I hate when he calls Artie or me "son". I'm sorry he lost his son, and maybe because of that it makes me extra uncomfortable that he does.

"Feels good to be outside and not wet," I say.

He nods and ambles off toward the woods. He keeps looking along the ground, always searching, as if he's he lost some small object.

Suppose he could be searching for animal tracks. That would be logical. But what if he isn't and he's looking for human tracks, and he's paranoid?

I scour the mountainside, not far from here. We have to make it over that? Is there another way? Artie won't make it over the ridge. I pull my feet from the clenching grip of mud and turn back. I have to get to Artie before he returns.

"Hey, Art. It's stopped raining. We have to get out of here. How's your foot?"

He gradually lifts his head as if he's drugged. He's completely dazed.

"Art, come outside. You need fresh air."

"O-kaaay." He stands up, and tips sideways, catching his balance on the chair.

"You gotta put some weight on that foot. Get it working again."

"Yeah, it's pretty sore."

"Where's your shoe?" We have to hurry.

"Oh,... yeah." Artie moves like a sleepwalker.

"Hold up. I'll get it." I race over to the drawing table and search underneath. "Here it is, hurry. He'll be back any second."

Artie's moving much too slow. I squat down and help him stick his foot into the sneaker; he holds both my shoulders, reminding me of the days after Mom died when Rick couldn't or wouldn't help us. He pretty much had me take care of Artie, and get him ready for school, feed him, and make his lunch. I know what Artie eats. I leave his laces loose. His body's stiff. He doesn't cry out, instead, he clenches down on my shoulders, digging deep into my collarbone.

"Where're you two going?"

I jump and almost knocking Artie over. "Get some fresh air, while it's not raining," I tell him.

"No, you aren't." His face is like a wolf, furry, and rigid, ready to attack.

My blood runs cold. We're trapped. Anger rises up through my chest. I grab Artie's arm.

❧ 7 ❧

The old man throws a pile of roots on the desk. "It's raining again. Looks like you boys're stuck with me, maybe overnight by the looks of things." He smiles in his weird way. "For a little while longer, anyway."

I stand at the cave opening. There it is, the never-ending rain, pouring down. Flooding will be everywhere. It's a wonder the cave hasn't already.

"With the global warming the rain never seems to stop anymore," the old man says. "The Earth, she's cleansing herself, cleaning everything up and out." He rubs his furry face and stifles another cackle.

I check in with Artie. "You want your shoe off again?"

"Yeah, It hurts more with it on."

I help him remove the shoe. He hobbles back to the desk and resumes his reading assignment inferred by our captivating host.

Defeated. I notice a cot up against the far wall, lined with pillows. I'm tempted to go lie down, but there's no telling what lives in that mattress. So I sit on the stool next to the drawing table.

This is getting tiresome. I can't wait anymore. We have to get out of here and find our way back to the lodge. We have to tell the police about the bomb. We know most of the police in Warren Country, from Gravelsburg to the lodge, here in Neumanville. I glance around, with that 'up against the wall' exhaustion, numbing my thoughts.

"Hey, Jackson. Listen."

Artie turns the radio up.

. . . if you see them, please contact the Sheriff's office. Both boys last seen near Teller's Ridge along Eagle's Creek.

"They're looking for us," he says.

"Good. Hey, Gunther, you got any flares, stuff like that?" I ask.

"Hell, all we need to do is make a fire. Once the rain stops. I'll be right back. I forgot something. You kids stay put. No sense going out in this weather."

All I can think is, the rain's never going to stop. Ever. It could rain for two weeks straight and often does in early April, the month of unending sog and sludge. I'm about to climb the walls. I can't hang here another minute. The dampness rattles in my chest when I cough. The exhaustion from not sleeping all night, lying over tree roots and pine bristle, with ants crawling over me, and the smell of deer's blood draining into the bucket, my nerves and patience are less than thin. But I have to keep calm. I have to take care of Arthur, take control, and get us out of here. Please, make Brianna have waited at the lodge for us, and not go to the Shop & Save to get Rick supplies, just to be kind. God, I hope she stayed at the lodge. I repeat it over and over in my head, but it doesn't calm me.

Artie catches my eyes. I give him a look he'll understand. It reads: We're getting out of here. He drops his eyes away from me, and descends into Thoreau.

Percolating entrails spread like a rubber glove over the room, squeezing me with its dirty sock stench. It mixes with the pinching odor of wild onions and waves in and out with the breeze. Mom would cook offal stew after some of Rick's hunts.

She didn't eat it, but she didn't want to waste the organs, either. Only he and his friends ate the stew.

He comes up and grabs Mom from behind. She starts laughing like she's being tickled. He holds up a brown paper bag. "Keep that stinky thing away," she says.

"Okay," he laughs and throws the soggy paper bag into the sink. His hunting friends filter away into the living room.

"Maybe you prefer this then?" He swings her around and pulls a small box from his pocket.

"What's this?" she asks.

"The surprise."

Mom's face shines. Her smile rises so far I can't see her eyes anymore. "You didn't?"

"I did." His laugh is deep and strong, and comforting. The way it used to be.

She opens the box, and in an explosion of happiness, she throws her arms around him. When they pull away, Mom remembers that I'm sitting at the kitchen table and Artie walks in.

"Boys, look, isn't it beautiful." She turns to our dad. She's crying.

He takes the old band off her finger and turns to us. "You kids are witnesses to this." And he replaces it with the new ring, stating that he loves her, in sickness and in health, and the rest of all that. They kiss.

One week later we get a call from her doctor.

THE POT SIMMERS at the entrance of the cave. That isn't dangerous at all. It's not as if there's a fire escape at the back of the cave.

Or is there? What if the old man needs an escape? If say, his plans didn't work out, and he was found hiding here, and became surrounded by police officers? He'd have to bolt and fast.

I lift myself from the stool and ease over to the bookshelf near the cot. More books, mostly philosophy, I run my hand over them: Friedrich Nietzsche, Michel Foucault, Noam Chomsky,

Robert Paul Wolff, Carl Jung, and Karl Marx. I know some of the authors, having read a couple of their books for school. Gunther seems to be a well-read man, and probably intelligent, once — until he decided to take down the Worthington Center.

A small alcove is to the right of the cot, where a plastic shower curtain hangs from a dowel. Turning first to make sure Gunther isn't standing behind me, I pull the curtain back.

A passage. I bet it leads to an exit. And there, sitting at my feet I discover the supplies for his bomb. Of course, I know what they are. Common things you can buy around town without anyone lifting an eyebrow. He's definitely making one. If he hasn't already, the acetate, and pool cleaner, giant milky tubs filled with something, are heavy, and unmarked, sitting, ready for their purpose. It's proof.

It's not only the drawings that incriminate him. We have to get out of here tell everyone about the bomb.

"Got some wild parsnips," the old man shouts.

I almost pull the curtain down.

"...For our dinner. And I found some extra wild potatoes for you Arthur. They're a little small, but no matter."

Hunger bears down on me, even the offal begins to smell edible. I never eat deer meat. I'll never forget the one I shot or the look in its eyes. My head's a mess, conspiring with my stomach to wear me down. I need strength now, for Artie, and for me. I need to eat. I expect Artie won't touch the innards. Good thinking, Gunther, parsnips for our vegetarian. He gets it. How come Rick doesn't?

"The stew's almost cooked. I'll set the parsnips on the fire, like so, and in ten minutes we can eat everything and feel strong again." He leaves the parsnips and strolls over to the deer. He surveys his work. "Jackson, could you give me a hand, again?"

I meet him at the stinking carcass.

"They're looking for us. You heard them on the radio." I wasn't about to mention that our father's a cop in Gravelsburg.

"Great. That's gotta make you feel better?" he says in a steady voice.

"Yeah."

"Hold still."

Peeling downward, he rips the skin from the deer. I use the last of my energy to keep the deer from banging against either of us, until he's pulled the last stubborn piece away.

"There. Free at last. Don't know where I can dry this ... ah, I know." He takes the sad sheath over to the cave opening and hangs it on a protruding rock near enough to the fire for drying.

Spring onions and mint diffuse the rank sewer stench for now. It'll get worse.

"Shouldn't be much longer. Getting hungry?" the old man asks.

Artie lifts his head, looking weaker than ever.

"You, young man, must eat," he commands.

I have to agree with that.

Artie stands and stretches, arching his back, and limps over to the fire where Gunther stands, with the recently washed metal tray. Suppose he uses the stream when he leaves. *The water source.*

That's it! That's how we'll find our way back.

The stream with the trillium flowers must make its way down here. Of course. Artie and I have to follow the water upstream.

❦   8   ❦

The old man hands me a plate with a blob of deer heart, pieces of liver, and burnt parsnips. He hands Artie a plate with parsnips and two small twisted potatoes.

"Want some deer heart, Arthur?" he asks, with that loopy smile of his.

Artie opens his mouth, I swear he's about to give in, but he declines. I suppose with Rick's idea of vegetables, the potatoes and parsnips are a hearty meal.

"How's your foot?" he asks.

"It's still sore."

"We should get another look at it. After we eat."

Artie nods and picks up a parsnip with his fingers, the blackened tops hang from the end.

"Do you have a clock around here?" I need to know the time. Rick must be worried. There'll be a search team after us, but they aren't going to find us. Not here. I don't think the old man hears me, or he has selective hearing. He's busy filling his plate.

Too hungry to think and too hungry to care I push my repulsion aside and dig in. The taste of wild onions hits first. Sure appreciate that. I savor the mint.

The liver is sweet and oniony. He knows how to kill a deer. Rick's usually a good shot. Not that I know from eating it, but his friends usually let us know if the kill was clean and fast to the heart. If a deer dies before knowing it's been shot, he dies fearless and quick, without contaminating the taste. Opposite of what happens when it's shot the wrong way. I swallow the lump of venison heart. "There's a stream nearby?"

"Yeah, not too far from here. It's where I found your dinner," he says and sits down.

"You must have shot this deer clean. Tastes pretty good, though, I'm no deer eater." I survey my empty plate.

The old man laughs at my irony. Or I think he is.

"Didn't need a shotgun. Snuck up and snapped its neck."

Not sure why it bothers me, Rick wasn't one to shy away from coarse details. But after he says it, I move on to the parsnips. I didn't get any potatoes; guess there're only enough for Artie.

"We're going to see if the stream'll take us over the mountain," I announce, and wait, chewing the parsnip.

"Yeah, it does. All the way to East Point, ... but it's too wet. Remember what happened already? Things could get worse, and your brother, he should stay dry."

I still get the feeling he doesn't want us to go. He's right, though, Artie should stay dry. Maybe the old man's lonely. If I hung around a cave day in and day out, with only my hunt for company, I'd sure be lonely.

"Do you have a CB radio?"

He wipes his mouth with the bloody rag from his pocket. The coarseness of his beard bristles against the fabric. When it's quiet, every stir in this hollow rock bounces from each wall. He sits there, chewing, and stares at me for a few seconds too long, and then at Artie. "No. No, I don't." He shakes his head.

I finish eating, and notice Artie hasn't. "Can I have your potatoes?"

He lowers his plate, and I snap up the two twisted tubers and throw them into my mouth. Cannot let a single source of edible energy go to waste. We're getting out of here. Tonight.

"Let's see that foot of yours," Gunther says, sounding concerned.

Artie lifts his foot, and he takes the sneaker, which has been a resting spot for his toes from the damp ground, and unwraps the bandage.

"It's very swollen. The wound looks fair. I'm gonna get more antibacterial cream and a clean bandage, this one's damp. Hold on. Jackson, back by the cot there's a shelf on the bottom with a first aid kit. Can you get it? I'll hold Arthur's foot till we can rewrap it."

He wants me to nose around his bins and shelves. Great. I'll take inventory. We can redress Artie's foot and get out of here.

I find the bin easily. "Here." I pass the box to him and walk over to the cave opening.

The rain has stopped. How long would it last this time? There are breaks in the sky. Streams of blue in-between the grey. It's dark blue, and later than I thought. Do I risk leaving this late? I know Rick and the others are out looking for us. They have to be, especially now that it's stopped raining.

I don't want to confront Gunther. He knows we want to go home. He can't expect we'll stay here indefinitely.

Of course, I have no way of knowing what he thinks. So far as I know his thoughts are extreme, and now that we know about his plan to make a bomb, he'll have good reason to keep us here.

Artie and I have to make a break for it, the next time he heads out. We have to be ready.

I concentrate my glare at Artie, while he finishes the last wrap around his foot. Artie's in pain, but he endures it. Like when Doctor Milton gives us shots, I'm the one who winces and grumbles loud enough Artie can hear me in the waiting room.

"There that should keep dry for awhile. This damp cave is not good for you to spend so much time in."

That's my cue. It's time to leave.

"There, Arthur, you sit tight and keep your leg up. Shouldn't get too much worse," he tells him. But Gunther gives me a questionable glance. I didn't get a second view of Artie's foot, but it couldn't be much better. Is Artie strong enough to make the trip over the mountain? He has to be.

He brings Artie a drink. "Keep hydrated. All this water everywhere, easy to forget you haven't taken any in yourself. Drink." He holds a smile under his brush of whiskers. "There, there, good. You need to lift your foot and keep it dry, very important. I'm going to carry you to the cot. All right?"

Artie agrees. He hoists him up, the way he held the deer on his shoulder, and lays Artie onto the cot. He replaces the pillows, optimizing my brother's comfort. "The walls are cold. Keep the pillows separating you." He stands to full position. "I'm going out. You stay put, now. Don't you go walking on that foot, understand?" The old man looks at me, for much too long.

Artie nods silently, while I make other plans for us. Gunther turns and disappears behind the curtain. When he comes out, he has a rifle with him and leaves the cave.

I wait a few minutes, but Artie's about to fall asleep. "Art...?" I nudge. "You fall asleep faster than anyone I know. Artie?"

"Hmm? Jackson?

We gotta go," I whisper. "Now."

He grimaces. I'm sure it's in anticipation of the pain to come with our climb over the mountain. Artie will have to bear the brunt of it.

"Now?"

"Yes, he just took off with a shotgun and the rain stopped."

I check around for anything we can take with us. There isn't much. An old puffy coat hangs on a hook. I wrap Artie and snap the coat tight around him. It smells of mold. He doesn't want to put his arms in the sleeves and lies there, sweating. I feel his head; he's burning up.

No time to waste. I scour the plastic drawers: fishing tackle, needles, and repair kits, among other things. What should I take? Dry bandages. I grab two handfuls and stuff them into the puffer coat covering Artie. I search for food. But there's nothing. How long will it take for us to get over the mountain?

I lift Artie; groggy, and almost lifeless, he limps alongside me. At this pace, it'll take days.

There's a post against the wall and I give it to him, hoping it'll ease his walking. I peer out of the cave to make sure the old man isn't traipsing back. Gunther Antwerp now holds a shotgun in his hands.

❦ 10 ❦

The moon comes from behind the clouds in the east as we leave the cave, suggesting a direction. I hear the stream on my right, and the last of the rain, dripping from the leaves to the ground. The stream flows north, into North Woods.

We need to walk south, upstream.

The ravine we fell from will be east of here. I get my bearings, hold Artie to my arm, and trudge in that direction. I turn to the moon and beg it to stay out from behind the clouds until we make it to the lodge.

We don't move as fast as I expected, and I didn't expect much. But I practically have to drag Artie and his stick keeps digging into the ground. I walk zigzag for a little while, then straight, so the old man doesn't see the direction we've gone. But who am I kidding? He'll know exactly where we're going. He knows where our lodge is. He has a gun with him and we're practically going in slow motion. "Come on, this way. We have to follow the stream. It'll take us near the trillium."

Artie seems to be going in and out of consciousness. He's

heavy, like a deadweight ton, and his temperature is hotter than before. "It's a different way," I tell him.

I talk on and on, trying to keep Artie awake. "This will lead us to the lodge. Stay with me, Artie. Come on." I become impatient, lifting him along. I sense the old man finding our tracks. He'll come after us when he sees the oil all over the drawings.

We know about his plans. If he catches up with us, there's no telling what he'll do.

I knew Artie would have trouble walking, but I couldn't account for how excruciating it would be to drag him. He must have a pile of mud layered over his foot, plowing through the undergrowth. It's impossible to keep dry. When we break I'll give him a dry bandage. But we have to keep moving, that's first priority, even if it means leaving Artie's foot soaking wet for now. We'll clean it when we reach the lodge. We'll have a pharmacopoeia of antibiotics to choose from. Where it's warm and dry. I repeat some of this to Artie.

Even seeing Rick's face will be a comfort. Hearing his crazed laugh, laughing at one of his own jokes. That will be comforting. Brianna? Will she be at the lodge? Please be there. I want to hear her laugh, smell her strawberry shampoo, feel her heartbeat against my chest, her calming patience.

Artie hangs onto my arm, but his grip is loosening, he manages to hold onto the pole with his other arm. Every few minutes he makes an awful cry. I press on.

Under the thick trees the moon is out of sight. We no longer use it to guide our way. I follow the sound of the stream, listening for voices that might be calling our names. But there're none.

Where are the search parties? Rick should have officers from both Neumanville and Gravelsburg out looking for us, plus the Sheriff's office, why doesn't he? The radio did say they were searching for us. Are they still out looking?

I remember the sun setting, but how long ago was that? Did

the search parties go home to sleep in their dry beds after giving up?

"J-ack-son...Jack-son," Artie stutters.

"What?" I sound impatient, I don't mean to.

"I have to sit...I can't . . . "

He's at his limit, or well past it, I knew this several meters back. I try and find a dry place to rest that won't take us too far from the stream. So long as I can hear it we're good. If the old man comes looking for us he'll follow the stream, too. But it's all we have to go on. The stream tethers us to the lodge.

A clearing opens ahead. The moon shines for a few minutes at a time, winking glimpses of light.

"Wait here, Art." I lower him onto a rock. We've been heading upstream for over an hour, Artie needs rest. I listen for breaking branches, or the sound of footsteps. When the moon flashes its seconds' worth of light, I scour the area for any tall-ominous-gun totters, and catch a glimpse of a giant pine tree among a row of pines, and walk over to check it out.

I reach under the tree, hoping for a semi-dry refuge. This particular pine has a clearance that'll allow plenty of space to camouflage us. I run back for Artie. He's slumped over, nodding off.

I carry him on my back; limp, and crawl under first, wondering if we might disturb a nesting raccoon already there. I pull Artie in with me when I'm sure we're alone.

The ground is thick with pine needles. The needles should keep us from sinking into the wet underground. I remove Artie's puffer coat, so he can lie on top of it, and feel for his foot. It's wet. Probably not much use replacing the bandage now when it's only going to get wet again.

I crawl out from under the tree, take a stick and scrambled our tracks, and return to Artie. Hidden under the pine tree, we're safe from the old man, for now.

"Should I take the bandage off, give it some air?" I ask.

He doesn't answer and I can't see him. "Are you with me, Artie?"

He takes a hold of my wrist, and gives it the slightest squeeze. "Yeah," he whispers.

Not sure if it's a good or bad idea I open the bandage and leave it to air out. Wish we had the old man's radio. Should have brought it with us. That would have been smart.

"Think he's gonna come after us?" Artie asks.

"Most likely, when he finds out we've seen his drawings. "

"I mean, Dad?"

"You heard the radio. They sent out search parties."

"What if they gave up?" His voice is a whisper, and fading. I have to keep him talking, keep him from going unconscious.

"It hasn't been that long, Art. This rain would slow anything down. Bet the search parties won't stop just because the sun has set. We have to buck up and be strong." Soon as I say it, I realize it's for my own benefit. Artie's been nothing but strong. But there's no way Artie can survive another night out in the woods. Not sick.

"Where are the helicopters and search lights?" he asks.

"You can't get a chopper low enough in the woods. Impossible." I say, "They'll have flashlights, if they're out looking now."

"Search dogs?"

"Yeah, probably."

"What's that noise?"

I stop breathing.

I hear it, too, the crunching, branches being stepped on. I peer through the pine bristle. It's hard to see anything. I drop into the needles on the ground, as if they'll cover me. We're already well hidden. All I can think is the old man's found us.

The steps come closer.

"Wha—"

"Shh," I whisper.

It stops; the footsteps of whatever it is, stops.

Then it starts again, the crunching, the breaking branches. There's an odor, not unlike the scent of the rotting deer carcass.

A heavy thud hits the ground outside the parameter of the pine tree, and there's a growl. Then I see its outline through the branches. "A bear," I whisper. The bear tore into a deer foraging nearby.

"It must have followed us," he says.

"We can be glad the deer was closer."

Artie takes a clump of dirt and pine needles and rubs it over his exposed skin in a short burst of energy.

I might have laughed under other circumstances. "What are you doing?" I ask, though I can guess.

"He'll smell us."

"I don't think it'll be hungry enough after eating the deer to bother with us." I say, thinking it might be reassuring, and possibly true.

The bear stops eating.

I separate the pine branches to see what startled it.

There're voices. Deep men's voices and they're getting closer.

"You hear that?"

"Sounds like, Griff and ..."

"Yeah, where's the bear?"

A gunshot goes off.

"Are they out looking for us or hunting bears?" I say, with great relief.

It's Griffin and Paul Spence, arguing about missing an unmoving target. I see their lights. When they're close enough, and I'm sure they've scared the bear away I jump out, leaving Artie under the protection of the pine tree.

"Griffin. Mr. Spence!" I yell, twice.

"I hear Jackson—shut up!"

"Yeah! We're here. Artie and I are right here!" I flail my arms, trying to stand out of the shadows.

Their lamplights brighten as their shapes change into tall figures. "Jackson!"

"Yeah!" I wave more frantically.

"Where's Arthur?"

"He's under here. His foot's hurt, real bad."

"Damn, you kids. You're dad's sick with worry. Got the whole of Warren County out looking for you," Mr. Spence says.

"You found us, and you were looking for us, right?" I ask.

"Yeah, of course. But the bear was right there. Easy target," Griffin confesses.

"Yeah, but you missed." Mr. Spence corrects him, and helps me reach under the tree for Artie, trying to crawl out.

"Hey, Griffin, help lift Artie on my back. Never mind. Take the rifle. Jackson, can you hike him up? That's it. Good. How you feeling kid?"

He doesn't answer and drops his head on Mr. Spence's back. Surrendering, just as relief arrives.

Mr. Spence takes his radio. "Spence here, we have the kids. Heading back to the lodge for our vehicles. Arthur's hurt, foot injury. Over and out."

Paul Spence is stronger build of the two, and much older than Griffin, though carrying Artie's lanky limbs wouldn't be a problem for either of them.

We begin the trek, over the rocks and stream, through the dark, guided by Griffin's lantern. I hold one in the rear, and every few seconds, check behind me for the old man. Artie's moving in and out of consciousness and releases a tremor of groans.

WE PASS A CLEARING, or two, and I see a few stars.

If it weren't for the bear I wonder if Griffin and Mr. Spence would have found us, or if we'd have made it out of the woods at all. It's possible the bear followed us until it found the deer as the prime choice over struggling with two boys.

After carrying Artie over every rock and ditch, Mr. Spence hands him over to Griffin to take over. "Your girlfriend's at the lodge, says she isn't going anywhere till she sees you," he tells me, supporting Artie onto Griffin.

"Yeah?" I say, relived. But then I imagine Brianna alone with Rick all those hours. Left to talk. Would she tell him?

My anxiousness to get back turns to agitation. It hangs in my throat and won't budge. We have to move faster.

But Bri wouldn't tell him anything without asking me first. Two days in the woods and I'm already losing it. I keep watch of Artie, dozing off, with his head bopping up and down. "Almost home, getting closer," I whisper. Anything, that'll help him hang on.

These guys sure know the woods, and should, considering they've lived at East Point all their lives. They're cops too, and the ones who got Rick to invest in the lodge.

We stand at the foot of the ravine. Mr. Spence traces the drop with his flashlight. The stream rushes over the cliff. I watch each of their faces in the lamplight.

Disorientation holds me in its grip. The half-moon, above, reflects more light I've seen in days.

"You boys fell from there?" Griffin asks.

"Somewhere along there, yeah." I peer around, wondering if Gunther's out there, hidden in the dark. Waiting to make his move.

"It's a treacherous climb." Mr. Spence analyzes. "And it's dark. Hard to see how the rocks are positioned."

"Is there another way? You must know another pass back. Don't you?"

"Here, buddy, sit a minute," Griffin says, setting Artie carefully onto a rock.

"Let me think about this," says Mr. Spence.

Artie's condition looks worse. His face contorts from the pain, and he speaks, but it's nothing intelligible.

"How bad is it, Art?" I ask, hoping he'll understand me.

"Can't feel . . . my leg."

Worse than I thought. Of course it's worse than I thought; his foot's infected. I become frantic. We have to hurry.

"How'd you guys get down?" Griffin asks.

"We rolled down, remember. I told you, that's how Artie ripped his foot in the bear trap. Can't we follow the stream back?"

"This is it. The stream falls over the rim of that ravine. But I have a rope." Mr. Spence assures me.

"You have a rope?" I make a mental note: always travel with a rope, and a flashlight, when heading into North Woods.

Artie cries out, letting loose the pain he's been holding down. Maybe there's some relief in crying out. I sure hope so.

"Where's Rick?" I ask.

"You mean your dad?" Mr. Spence says. "He's sick with worry." He's already sick.

"But where is he?" I want to hear Mr. Spence tell me he's drinking his worries away in a bar, like usual. The truth.

"He and Jumper are scouring the highlands," Griffin answers, behind the darkness. I want to believe it.

"Look, Jackson, your dad's got all of Gravelsburg and Neumanville's officers out hunting for you," Mr. Spence says, while throwing the grappling hook up the ravine. He tosses it a few times before it latches onto anything secure enough to take our weight.

Artie only utters what's necessary, and the only thing necessary is a grunt or moan, reminding us of his agony.

"Okay kid. You ready? Arthur?" Mr. Spence waits until Artie turns his head toward him. "I'm going to hook you on my back, with this belt. It's very secure."

Griffin helps attach Artie onto Mr. Spence. His legs hang loose, and Artie starts mumbling again.

"Hey kid, if you wanna break out the F-word I understand," Mr. Spence says.

"F . . . " Artie whispers, like it's his last breath.

"Guess it means more to me than you. Okay." Mr. Spence knots the rope around him. "Now hold on, real tight."

"Ahhhh!" Artie shrieks.

I notice Artie's foot has no support, and he's about to be dragged and bumped over brambles and stones.

"Wait!" I shout.

Mr. Spence stops. "Griff, anything we can use to protect the kid's foot?"

Griffin rustles through his bag and pulls out duct tape.

"Duct tape?" I ask, directing the lamp his way.

"Yeah. Here's a flashlight, take it," he says. "We gotta get creative here.

"I'll look for branches."

"See, now you're thinking. Thinking's good," he says. As if he'd know. I give him a few sticks, and hold the light. He makes a splint for Artie's foot, behind a wall of sticks and duct tape. Then he wraps the rope under his knee, which Artie can use as a lever to pull his leg higher. Artie will have to hold the rope through the worst of it, all the way to the top of the ravine, all thirty yards of it.

"Good, Arthur?" Mr. Spence asks.

Artie mumbles. He's not good at all. I keep the flashlight on them.

"Hold on, Artie. I'm gonna start the drag. Can you raise your foot above the rocks?"

I wait for his answer. But he doesn't say anything. How can we expect he'll use the pulley to raise his leg?

Then Artie whispers, "Yeah . . . "

Artie's a fraction off the ground, tied to the back of Mr. Spence like a baby bunting. Mr. Spence begins to pull their way up the ravine. But they're not steady. He stops after a few steps and checks on Artie. Artie doesn't scream. I wish he would. Mr. Spence continues.

Watching them climb the mountain, rips at my gut. I can't take it. They're moving so slow. I search around, sensing the old man.

They're near the top, Mr. Spence stops. Says it's for a breather. I steady the flashlight. He's about the size of a cat from where I am.

Mr. Spence starts the climb again, pulling and wrenching, hand over hand.

They make it.

I watch as Artie's lowered to the ground. The rope comes back down.

"Jackson, you see where the rope went?"

I swing the flashlight in the general direction. Griffin walks over and searches.

"It's there. Right over there." I flash the light again.

"Teamwork," he says. "Remember?"

"Yeah, I hold the light, and you're supposed to watch where it goes."

Griffin reaches into the weeds. "Okay, smarty. Here." He hands it to me. "It's already attached, just start climbing. I'll take the flashlight now, and the lantern. You're gonna need two hands."

I hurry up the ravine as fast as I can. Hand over hand, over rock and stone, and one sneaky loose stone. I hold tight. When I reach the top, I throw the rope down to Griffin.

He hooks the lamp on his belt and comes right up. I offer to carry my brother. I owe him this. I need to feel him, and carry his weight. Carry some of his pain. They give in and allow me to carry him some of the way back. I wonder about Gunther, and if he watched us climb over the ravine? Knowing we're that much closer to the authorities, and he's that much closer to being caught?

We reach the trillium flowers, at the start of the trail that leads to the creek, but we aren't going that way. We're close to the lodge, and in East Point. Our ordeal is over.

I lower Artie to the ground once we reach Eagle's Stone Ridge. Mr. Spence takes over and carries him.

The lights in the lodge are on. The door swings open. Brianna runs toward us, her long hair in tangles flying behind her. "Oh my God!" She wraps her arms around me. Her warmth almost shuts me down.

"Artie's hurt," is all I can say, and keep moving.

"Your father's out looking for you," she says, following our convoy into the lodge.

Mr. Spence brings Artie to the couch. The first real light reveals red splotches on his face and patches along his arm. He's semi-conscious. Mr. Spence peels back Artie's ripped pants for a better view. I almost say something, but hold back for Artie's sake.

Not Brianna. "No-no-no! That's an infection." Her hands cover her mouth. She's been crying. Her eyes are bloodshot. I know she cares very much for Artie, too.

"We gotta call the ambulance," Griffin says.

"Ambulance? I'm driving to the hospital." Mr. Spence lifts him. Artie's head hangs like a goose waiting for slaughter. "Call both stations," he yells to Griffin. "Tell the guys to find Rick. We're going to Truman Hospital."

"I'm coming, too" Brianna announces. "I'll drive my car. Jackson, you coming with me?"

"I have to stay with Artie."

She nods like she understands, but her arms wrap her stomach as if she's in pain, the center of her despair, reminding me of our connection and our shared loss.

She runs to her green Honda, saying she'll follow us. Mr. Spence has Artie. Artie isn't talking. His eyes are shut tight; his head bobs with each step. I reach out and steady him.

I dared to look at his foot, swollen with puss, covered in dark red spots and deep gouges. Infection has set in. How bad, I don't know. I'm scared, real scared, thinking Artie could die from the infection. This is worse than thinking the old man will come after us, worse than worrying about Rick's anger or losing a baby that would have been born this April. I'm about to retch, but there's no time for self-pity. I can't lose Artie.

"Artie, stay with us," Mr. Spence says.

I grab his searing hot hand. "Stay with me, Artie! Hang on—you gotta hang on. We're taking you to the hospital. We're out of the woods," I tell him, wondering if Gunter would be far behind, if he followed us.

I keep demanding he stay with me and not give up. I keep talking. Telling him about the bear, telling him how pine needles don't mask the odor of boys. I know Artie's strong. Stay strong, Artie, I need you.

He's strong enough to always be himself. He's strong enough to know what he needs, strong enough to care about small, injured birds, or bears. Or anything, no matter what anyone else says—and he was strong enough to survive Mom slipping out of our lives a little each day.

∾

"STAY WITH ME, LITTLE BROTHER." Artie's hand goes limp.

Mr. Spence lays Artie across the back seat and straps him in. I settle his hand over his hip and get in front with Mr. Spence. Griffin drives his truck behind us. Brianna's back there, too.

"Don't worry, your dad will meet us at the hospital, soon as he gets the message."

I wonder if Mr. Spence might be saying this to comfort Artie. "The doctors are gonna take real good care of you," he says. "You'll see. Don't you worry," he turns, saying that last part to me.

I'm sure Artie hears none of it. He's out.

We screech to a stop. Mr. Spence pulls Artie from the back seat and I follow. I don't wait for Brianna.

I repeat over and over, "Everything's going to be fine...everything's going to be fine."

She collapses, said she was tired. Dad wasn't home, and I help her to bed. He wanted Mom at the hospital, somewhere she could get the help she needed. It was time. I started calling the house from school to hear her voice. I had to hear her voice, I didn't know if she'd be there when I got home.

HE GOT THE CALL. I see Rick through the glass doors, standing with his arms folded under the flickering light; waiting for a confrontation and wearing a white bandage on his cheek.

We burst through the ER. Rick's face is pink and prickly, signaling where he spent his last few hours' recreation. Sure, maybe he was worried, but Mr. Bower can't live without some things—and some things, aren't necessarily us.

"Dad!" I yell. I won't lie, there's some relief seeing him, and thinking he might be glad to see me. But emotions take a long time coming for Mr. Rick Bower.

His eyes brush past me without any discernable feeling, before they settle on Artie. Rick's face grows tight with what might be anger, or worry, but I wouldn't know the difference.

One might think him, a kind, responsive father the way his face freezes after seeing Artie's foot, like a gust of wind has taken his breath. He cups Artie's face and lifts it into the light. Artie's eyes open, barely, and he mutters something. Rick nods.

Mr. Spence holds Artie until the stretcher finishes its way over, then he lowers him, reminding me of how Artie cradled the baby bird into its nest. This motion seems to invoke a protective barrier, a shield of protection.

"Sepsis -- blood poisoning," Mr. Spence whispers to Rick.

He didn't want to say it, and none of us wants to hear it. The nurses whisk Artie away. Rick follows.

Brianna's right arm comes from behind and tucks undermine. "I'm so sorry, Jackson."

WE MOVE into the waiting room. Brianna sticks so close, we should probably get a couch, but she loosens her grip, and we separate over two pink plastic chairs. Mr. Spence and Griffin sit across from us.

"Where were you two?" Mr. Spence asks. "You were gone overnight."

Feels like we've been gone for days. Would have been two, if Gunther hadn't taken off with a shotgun in his hands.

I'm sure he's wanted to ask since finding us, unless the idea dawned on him this moment, having time to compile the scene in his head.

"No wonder, Artie's sick," Griffin says, chirping behind his question. "You guys sleep in the rain?"

"We were in a cave."

"A cave?" Griffin echoes.

Brianna hasn't said much, and she's usually a good talker. Instead, she lets her eyes do all the work and shoots me a horrified look.

I hesitate, not sure why.

All I could think of before was getting out of the cave, and telling the authorities about Gunther Antwerp's plans. I've engrained his name, so I won't forget. But my words hang back, and I can't figure how to lay them out. I think about Gunther, bandaging Artie's foot, feeding him roots.

Things our own father can't do. What would have happened if the old man never found us in the morning, and a bear found us, instead?

Or if Artie and I, both, came down with hypothermia? As I think about this, I realize the consequences for Gunther, in most cases, is death.

Then I remind myself about the civilians working at the Worthington Center and feel worse, and suddenly I can't breathe. I open my mouth and can't find the words, where do I start?

The innocent, faceless people of Worthington Center have nothing to do with Gunther's injustice. They will not pay with their lives.

"Some old man found us," I begin. "Sleeping under a tree in the morning, and took us to his cave."

Griffin's face contorts into a terrified expression. Brianna catches it, and after a minute, expresses the same sentiment on her face. She squeezes my hand.

"He didn't do anything to us," I tell them. "He was actually trying to help us."

"Didn't do a very good job with Arthur's foot," Mr. Spence says.

"No. Well, he tried. Think it got worse after we escaped."

"Escaped? Where's his cave?" Griffin asks.

"I don't know, how I can tell you? We were completely lost, and it was dark. I don't know North Woods like you guys."

"You know to follow the stream south, right?" Mr. Spence strains his voice.

"Yeah, sort of, and the stream falls over the cliff, and that's what we did. We went over the cliff. Only we didn't have a rope or a flashlight."

"So, who's this old man?" Griffin asks. "Some hermit?"

"Yeah."

"And he didn't try to hurt you or Artie? In my experience, an old man in a cave, deep in the woods has it out for someone. Some loony, no doubt," Mr. Spence says.

"He's not really old, just looks old."

Griffin shakes his head. I pull back what I want to say, but who am I protecting? Maybe they won't actually find Gunther, not with a hundred or more caves in North Woods. Would they?

"The old man didn't seem loony but . . . " I know they're right. He's loony, but he's also in pain, deep and agonizing pain.

"He's making a bomb." The words drop from my mouth like the bomb they are, and hang in front of us, reverberating: *He's making a bomb . . . he's making a bomb.* As if they can be retracted before any of them believes what they've heard.

Brianna shrieks; both her arms entangle me. I hold my breath for the onslaught of questioning.

"A bomb?" Mr. Spence whisper-shouts. "He plans to set a bomb off? Where? And you waited to say anything?"

Everyone in the waiting room begins to eavesdrop.

Griffin opens his phone. "Reception." He turns to Mr. Spence for approval. "I'm calling the precinct, . . . about an old man in a cave, who's building a bomb. You don't mind, do you, Jackson?" Griffin asks, his voice low. He gives me an odd glance. Thinks I'm covering for the old man, senses my hesitation. There's only so much you can hide from these guys.

Rick comes out of ER. "Arthur's going to be all right. They pumped him full of antibiotics. You hungry, Jackson?" He rests a heavy hand, with half his weight on my shoulder. "We should get some food."

I agree. Rick notices Brianna sitting next to me and nods to her.

"I can wait here, with Artie," she says.

"Jackson has something to tell you," Griffin says, pocketing his phone. They ask Rick to meet them right after at the Neumanville Station. I'm still reeling from the shock of telling Griffin and Mr. Spence. They say goodbye after telling Rick I have something to tell him, and ask him to meet them right after at the Neumanville Station. I know I'll have to be a witness in how this plays out.

Artie would do the same. He would. Then why do I feel so awful? I couldn't save an unborn baby. Although Brianna and I eventually agreed on what to do, I'll never forget, and I can't go back.

"We'll pick up from Dahlia's. Arthur requests pizza. We'll bring him the whole pie." Rick clips his sentences; he's exhausted. I wonder if he's been up all night worrying, or drinking?

He asks me to meet him outside, in a moment of sensitivity for me, and Brianna. I turn to her. "Sure you wanna stay here?"

"Where else would I go? I was right to be worried about you. I'll call my mom, tell her you're back and I want to stay."

"She's going to let you stay?"

"Jackson, she knows how much I care for you . . . and after I almost lost you." She squeezes my hand. "But you're here now."

She doesn't say love, never has, maybe never will. How long can we go on? I care for Brianna. But the two of us have lost our steam. Our shared pain, and my regret, poisons us. I just don't know how to let go. The way Rick does. He allows the people he once loved to pass through his life like ghosts.

"I'll be here when you get back," she whispers.

I kiss Brianna, even though Rick can see us through the window, and hurry out to meet him at the truck.

"Where the hell were you two?" he asks the moment I sit inside. Rick's regular voice returns, and he doesn't know about the bomb, yet.

His cell phone rings.

"Really? No, he did not. Okay, you do that. I'll see if I can get the logistics."

Rick shoots me an ugly, sour expression. "Some crazy old man had you and Arthur held up in a cave?" He wipes his dripping nose.

"We found out about it from the mechanical drawings he tried to hide. Labeled USAF, with every detail on how to build one." I wait a minute because I know it's not enough to incriminate a man. I continue, "I also saw some of the supplies. The usual bomb-making stuff." I list a few and where I found them.

"Did he do anything?" He's angry.

I know what he's getting at. "No, nothing. He fed us, and wrapped Artie's foot. I don't think he was planning on keeping us. Just kind of helped out.

"Did you see any actual bombs or just the supplies? He must have told you something."

"The drawings said, Worthington Center."

"It's planted there?"

"I'm not sure. I'm guessing he hasn't. The tubes were heavy. They were full."

"How would you know, Jackson?" He turns to watch the road. "We'll find him.

Rick gets on his radio and tells the police department in Gravelsburg to help the Neumanville precinct search the Worthington Center for bombs and the suspect. I give him a description. Then he calls Mr. Paul Spence. The Worthington Center is between Gravelsburg and Neumanville and about ten minutes away from here.

"I'll be there, soon as I can." Rick hangs up.

12

Rick pulls back the curtains surrounding Artie's bed. It's almost 10:00 PM. Brianna sits in the chair next to him, asleep with a book. She wakes up slowly.

Artie stirs.

"Pizza," I whisper, holding the steamy pie, loaded with vegetable toppings, which I demanded Rick add. I leave it on the table. Rick gets a call and takes a slice, and his conversation, out of the room. He mouths something about being right back.

"Hey—how you feelin'?" I ask Artie.

Artie opens his eyes, and his face lights up. A tube rests under his nose for oxygen, while another goes from his arm into a bag of fluid. His color has returned to somewhere near normal pale. "Hungry as a bear," he croaks. "Brianna's been bringing me cheese crackers from the vending machine. They ran out of nuts."

She smiles, her golden-red hair laces around her head, in the illusion of a halo. She doesn't have the usual strain on her face. She looks peaceful.

The same as that day last September, lying on the cot at the Community Center Clinic.

"Jackson, you're the most thoughtful person I've ever known."

"Yeah, you're talking about all my worrying?"

I hold her hand, soft, and warm. She's always so warm. I want to crawl under the sheet and take her place. I don't want her to have to go through this, alone. Accidents do happen, what if this clinic was a mistake? We had to drive a hundred miles for a decent doctor.

"No, silly," she whispers, fading in and out. They've given her something.

"... And the way you take care of Artie ... he's lucky to have you."

"What about you?"

"I'm lucky to have you too ... " Her eyes drop away from me.

A nurse asks me to sit in the waiting room. I don't want to let go of her hand. She's pulled away and her form blends into the white sheets until the door closes.

I ADJUST Artie's headboard so he can sit up and eat.

"The antibiotics have kicked in and working very well," Brianna says. "The nurses keep me updated. They said it's lucky he was treated right away."

The red spots on his arms are fading. Artie's eyes brighten each time he turns, seeing Brianna still with us. I hand him a slice. He gives me a reassuring nod.

"He's hungry, she says, "always a good sign." She puts the book down and stands over the bed.

"You're really feeling better?" I ask him.

Artie rushes to clear his mouth. "He was here," he whispers.

"Who?"

"Gunther."

"Did you see him, Bri?" I ask, turning behind me toward the door.

"No, Artie didn't say anything to me about it. Maybe he came when I went out for snacks?"

I lower my voice. "Gunther was here? You're not hallucinating, are you?" I feel Artie's forehead.

"No. He came to check on me--and steal meds. Said he used to work in this hospital." He's chewing his pizza as if he weren't in any danger at all. My heart stops, Brianna shares her concerned face with me. I meet it.

"He was a doctor?" I ask,

"Not a doctor, a technician."

"And no one saw him?"

"He was wearing scrubs and a mask."

Brianna makes an a-ha, with her eyes, maybe she saw him too?

I shake my head. I can't believe it. He's onto us. "Are you sure it was him?"

"I'm sure," Artie says. "We talked. We talked about the drawings."

My gut sinks, I feel sick, again. "He knows — of course, he knows." Now he's after us. The room starts to swerve.

"He's not going to do it," Artie says in full belief, raising his voice above a whisper.

"What? And you believe it?" I ask. "Did you convince him?"

"I guess."

"Where is he now?"

"Must have gone home." Artie reaches for another slice of pizza, while Bri helps him.

"To the cave? Rick and two precincts are out looking for his cave."

"Jackson, you gotta stop them. Tell Dad you lied about the whole thing."

"You mean about the bomb?"

"You've got to stop them. They'll kill him." Artie lowers his voice again. "Gunther swore he wouldn't bomb the center."

Brianna's tired, or in a state of semi-shock, if there is such a thing, but she's listening. Standing next to the bed, with the piazza box about to drop from her hands.

Rick storms in. "I gotta go," he says. "You have a ride home."

He looks at Brianna. "I'm going to the station." He bends over Artie. "I'll see you in the morning. Get some sleep."

And he leaves, like always.

"Hold on, Bri." I stand outside the room and call out to him. "Rick—Dad." He doesn't stop. Doesn't even look back. He has the phone pressed against his ear, talking, until he's out of sight.

I turn to Artie. "This isn't good."

"Not one bit. You gotta go, Jackson, they can't find the cave without your help, right?"

I run after him.

"Dad. I want to come!" He's almost through the double doors. Rick stops and pulls the cell phone away from his ear.

"I have to help you find the cave. I was there. You're not going to find it without my help—not in time, anyway."

He digests the thought while chewing his last bite of pizza. "All right Jackson, maybe you're right. But you'll have to stay with me at the station until the crack of dawn."

"They aren't going to let Brianna stay at the hospital overnight, can she sleep at the lodge?"

"Sure, you know where the key is."

I nod and follow in his tracks. I use his phone to call Brianna since there isn't any time to run back. She tells me they've already come in to tell her she has to leave. She's happy to stay at the lodge and return in the morning to be with Artie.

"Hurry up. I have to convince the guys in Neumanville we need your help. They do things a little different here."

I'm not completely sure what he means, guess it has to do with the bureaucracy of it all since Neumanville is not his station.

The streetlights race past. What can I say that'll stop Rick in his tracks? He's not going to believe I lied about the bomb plot. Not now—he should; he doesn't know how often I do lie to him. Or maybe he knows and brushes it off, doesn't really care enough to deal with it. Doesn't want to deal with adolescent angst. Doesn't want to deal with me. Or deal with the fact that I have a girlfriend, who has a name. Certainly doesn't want to deal with Artie and his special diets; he just leaves me to deal with it.

"Can't the officers in Neumanville handle the situation? They're experts, aren't they? Mr. Spence, and Griffin, they'll know exactly where they found us. They know the woods better than you. Neumanville isn't even your jurisdiction." I wait.

He doesn't say anything. Is he trying not to? Is he merely making a plan, running ideas through his mind? I try again. "We should have stayed with Artie."

"He's in good care. There's an officer stationed right outside his room. Arthur's not going to die. I thought you were coming to help, Jackson. What's going on?"

"How would you know? You thought the same about Mom when you left us alone. When you left us with her calling for you." The words grip my throat. I wasn't expecting to go there. Rick looks at me, then through the rearview mirror, and pulls off the road.

First, he stares into his lap. He seems to melt, his shoulders slump forward; his face drops, and he grips the steering wheel. I half expect a slap across the face and brace myself.

"Jackson ... I loved your mother ... more than anything. She suffered for over a year; it was cruel and unfortunate that she passed right after I got that phone call. I had to leave. I was the one person who could identify the felon, the only witness. He was a very bad person. They would have had to set him free. Free to kill more people if I didn't identify him, immediately. I told you this. I guess it was hard to understand at twelve years old, suffering, yourself."

I can't see his face anymore. He's the formless blob cast on the other side of my wall of tears. I want to tell him every detail of the scene that's haunted me for the last five years, so it'll haunt him instead: Artie crying, me holding him, the nurses trying to comfort us, with no family around, and pulling us away from her bed; the replay of the empty feelings, the loss, facing the world alone. Mom told me to watch Artie. It gave me purpose to stand strong. Artie made me stronger. Maybe in the same way, Brianna has. I stayed by her side, holding us together.

"Artie wouldn't stop shaking her," I tell him. "He kept repeating, wake up momma, please, wake up. I had to pry him off her, screaming hysterically. That's when the nurses finally came in. Grandpa Bower didn't arrive for a long time. It felt like an eternity. I held Artie and promised Mom I'd never leave him."

I quickly wipe the tears dripping from my chin. "You never talked about Mom at all after that. She was gone, you made her gone for good."

He isn't looking at me. His grip stays tight on the steering wheel; his face hangs forward. When he finally lifts his head, I swear he has tears edging into his eyes. But he manages to keep them pushed away, the way he pushes most things away. He stares ahead, out beyond the windshield. Rick wouldn't let himself go, not now. Not on the way to a stakeout.

"Jackson ... I'm sorry ... my work, the pressure. I worry for you and Arthur. I know I put a lot of pressure on you to help and be my stand-in. I'm sorry, Jackson. Very, very sorry." Then he does what he normally does. He gets back to work.

"Right now, we need to catch that terrorist, find out if he's planted bombs in other places. And fast!" He starts the engine. This time he sticks the siren on the hood.

We race to the Neumanville precinct, going over 80 miles an hour. I turn away from him and stare out the window. My face reflects back at me, my eyes, swollen. I can't stop the tears, and I don't want him to see.

13

ARTHUR BOWER

Someone walks in. It's not the nurse and it's not Brianna. But I recognize the smell. He stands over me in scrubs, wearing the same mask the doctors wear. I know who it is. But I'm not afraid.

"Hi," I say and sit up.

"I wanted to check up on you Arthur, make sure you made it all right. They give you something for the pain?"

"Yeah, got some awful shots, too."

"Well, guess the worst is over. You're snug and warm. I was glad when I saw those guys found you before any wild animals did, like that the bear, which they missed." He shakes his head.

"You were watching us?"

"I wanted to make sure you made it home safe."

"What about those people, the one's working at The Worthington Center. It's not just a city building you know. There are moms and dads that work there. Somebody's mom and dad, maybe even one of my friend's mom or dad, and it's next to a grocery store. Everyone in town goes there. Kids too, Gunther. Children."

He sits on the chair next to me. The one Brianna's been sitting in and reading to me. She'll be right back.

"You care about much, don't you, Arthur. Just like my Anatole. You remind me so much of him at your age."

"I read the essay, *On The Duty Of Civil Disobedience*. I read most of the book. I read Walden, too."

"Yes, by Thoreau..."

"How can you do it? Thoreau would say: 'people have a duty to avoid allowing governments to make them into agents of injustice' but that's what you're doing. Anatole's death doesn't have to lead to destruction. Innocent people don't have to die and leave children without parents, or without sons or daughters, without love, without hope. You'd be doing the same thing. Can't you see? I'm sure, especially since you say we're so much alike, Anatole wouldn't want it, either. You said he cared about people ... and about life." I fall back on the pillow. It took every ounce of push, to get it out.

Gunther doesn't say a word. He sits, watching the floor.

"You okay?" I ask.

Tears roll down his face. "I made him go into the army, even though I knew better. I killed him. I killed my son." His eyes freeze, staring into space; maybe he's in shock, thinking this for the first time. He looks like a ghost and stays quiet.

After a few minutes, he says, "I forced him to enlist. But he got much worse than a bum leg, the way I did. It was my fault." Gunther's hands wipe his face; mixing tears into the hair hanging from the surgical cap. He can't contain his cries, and he's shaking..

"Shhh, the guard will hear you."

Nodding his head, he takes the handkerchief from his pocket and dries his face. Swallows a few breaths and sits there quietly. I listen, expecting footsteps to march down the hall and into my room. Or Brianna, she'll be back any minute.

His face changes, his eyes narrow and seem to cross inward, maybe seeing inside himself. He stands up. "Are you thirsty Arthur? Can I get you some water, soda?"

"Won't they see you?"

"Heck, I used to work here. Slipped right past that security guard in these scrubs — half asleep by the way. You should have stayed off that foot, Arthur, and kept it dry." He rubs his chin. "No matter, guess you'll be good as new soon."

"Were you a doctor?"

"No, a lab technician. I know, boring. Anyway, I better get going. Gonna grab some supplies before slipping out of here."

When he gets to the door, he turns to me.

"I'm not going to do it. I'm not going to bomb anyone or anything. You're right, and Thoreau has always been right. Which reminds me, I'd better get over there fast before Jackson leads the police to my home. I'll be lucky if I can pull a single book from the wreckage. I'll be back in the morning with a present for you. Thank you, Arthur."

He flips the surgical mask over his face and opens the door. He looks left and right and disappears.

❧ 14 ❧

I wait between the green and grey walls of the Neumanville police station. The flickering fluorescent lights irritate me. Feels like a freak show brewing. Officers scatter, dodging around me, others on their phones, snapping orders between them. I might have nodded off a few times, from the rhythm of it all, and the fact that it's almost midnight.

This isn't Rick's station, and getting the police together, and working on the "threat" takes longer than he wanted. But there isn't much they can do until dawn's light. They already have a bomb squad checking the Worthington Center.

Tension rises on Rick's face, turning it red with frustration. We wouldn't be going home to Gravelsburg, anytime soon, not with Artie still in the hospital, or with Rick on a mission to save the Worthington Center.

I watch the walls spin and try to figure out what I might say that he'd believe. How can I convince him the old man in the cave isn't going to bomb anyone? But how can I know for sure? It's what Artie said, and he's convinced. Do I tell Rick I lied to him? I'll get the beating of my life lying about a terrorist.

Rick hasn't hit me in a while, but once you get a smack across the face you half-expect another at any wrong move. A lie of this magnitude would warrant a heavy dose of reprimand. I shudder, thinking about it.

Save the people of Worthington Center or Gunther? It's really not much of a choice. If I protect Gunther I'll go down in the fray, though Artie wants me to help him now.

I watch Rick mentally prepare. As he focuses on the job, he barely acknowledges that I'm waiting on a bench.

I could lead them to another cave. But that wouldn't work. It'll be empty, and obvious that I misdirected them.

Rick comes over. "There's a cot inside. You wanna lie down? It's well past midnight."

"Guess I should."

"I could drive you to the lodge, but you'd be alone, and with that man out there...you probably told him where you're staying."

"Brianna's there." I almost forgot. "I have to call and check on her." I didn't really think the old man would do anything to her, would he?

"Use any of the phones."

Of course we told him where we were staying, we needed his help to find the lodge. "What are you gonna do?" I ask.

"We're going to get a team and move in on the cave, and with your help. You've always wanted to help at the station, now's your time. Remember we have to wake up before the sun does, so get some sleep."

I pull myself from the stool, and without saying anything else, move into the room with the cot. I use the phone to call the lodge. It's late. I'll wake her for sure, but I have to check. Now I wish I'd stayed with Brianna. The phone rings five times before she answers. "Hello?"

"It's me, Jackson."

"Are you all right?"

"I'm OK. Bri, do you want to meet me here at the station? It's right off the city limits, near route 49?"

"I'm asleep already. You want me to leave, now? Is Artie okay?"

"It's just, I'm worried. For you."

"Everything's locked, and there are about four guns in the mudroom. There's much worse to worry about now. You help your father get him. I'll be back at the hospital for breakfast. I promised Artie."

"You sure, it's not more than a ten-minute drive?"

"I'm not scared, Jackson."

There's silence. I want to say something but not sure what and then she says, "I'll see you in the morning, be careful." She says goodbye.

Rick comes in, carrying a drab, scratchy blanket, and lays it over me before he leaves.

I begin to drift off.

"Please, talk Jackson. It was a mistake. Don't blame yourself. Sometimes taking precautions doesn't work. That's a fact, we've learned. Now we can take responsibility and take the next step."

I didn't want to take the next step, but brooding about it wasn't going to help. It's her body after all. We didn't want a child, and we used a damn condom, but it must have broken seeing as my expertise on its application was below novice.

She's calling me out. I'm behaving just like him.

"You really want to do this?"

"We're seventeen, and sure not ready to start a family. I'm going to Monroe University in the fall. I'm not going to miss that chance—not like every other female in my family has. I've worked too damn hard, Jackson." She starts crying.

My body shakes as it jumps into sleep like I'm falling off a cliff, all over again.

❧   15   ❧

I jump up and rub my burning eyes; still at the police station, it wasn't a bad dream. The nightmare is real, and it coursed through the place: Boots pound the floor, figures rush past the glass door. Voices shout commands.

Rick's shadow stands behind the bottle glass for a minute before he opens the door. "There's not a lot of time," he says. "But here, some cocoa. It's all I could find. We've got five minutes. You okay with this? I know you wanted to come, and you might be the only person who can identify the cave and the terrorist, but you don't have to."

I nod. "Did they find any bombs at the Worthington Center?"

"No. Nothing. Most likely, he hadn't got them ready. Good work, Jackson. We'll get him when we find his cave — with your help." He tells me he'll be right back.

Pulling the blanket around my neck, I almost retch. The smell of the rain and dirt from the last two days covers me. I smell the deer carcass. Considering I haven't bathed, I still wear its blood.

I reach for the phone and dial the number for the lodge.

"Brianna!"

"Are you shocked?" she asks.

"No, just happy to hear your voice." Not sure what to say, but I feel better hearing her voice. Soft, like a song, lulling me, and lifting some of the weight riding my shoulders.

"I'm leaving when visiting hours open, Artie's been promised a veggie burger. You do what you have to do, Jackson. He'll be in good hands."

"Yeah, guess he will. If anything happens to me . . ."

"You're acting silly now. The entire police force of Warren County has your back."

Rick taps on the bottle glass.

"He needs me. I gotta go."

"I know. I'll see you soon."

We don't say goodbye.

He never needs anyone, but today he needs my help. I'll turn Gunther in if it means getting Rick's approval, a spark of recognition, some sign of acceptance. My help could save them time, not having to search each and every cave in North Woods. But I can't stop them. Artie's wrong about that. The wheels are in motion.

If there were a way to get to Gunther first and warn him I would. He could escape and I'd have nothing to do with it. I will have done my part.

I walk into the main area where the forces gather. Male officers and a couple of women, pull up the last of their riot gear, the clamor of weapons from their cases along the walls, rattle the room. Rick stands next to the Police Chief of Neumanville while he gives out orders. When he finishes, Rick walks over to me. "Let's go," he orders. "Follow close to me. The whole time—got it, Jackson?"

The rest of the soldiers load into the patrol wagons.

I sit in the police car behind Rick, who's in the passenger seat. Mr. Spence drives.

The firing squad is on the move, including me, the one who

ratted the old man out. The one who's going to get him killed because that's how these things go down. I have to figure out a way to warn Gunther.

$$\approx \quad 16 \quad \approx$$

A helicopter hovers above the police car. Not exactly going to surprise anyone. This is good. Gunther will hear the chopper and take off. The woods are thick with trees. Where does that thing plan on landing? If Gunther were to run out they wouldn't even see him. The trees offer some protection, some cover, but the dogs will smell him, and I know they've brought dogs.

Without much sleep the last couple days I feel sickness wearing into me, and the general guilt of possibly getting a man killed. Chills climb my spine, I'm cold, and the cough has settled into my chest. Not good.

Sniffles, shakes, and a sharp pain in my head seize me. Great Jackson, I think, Stay tight. Keep clear. Or you're going to screw this up. But how can I help Gunther get away? It's ridiculous to consider. It's not possible.

Rick hears my sniffles and turns to me in the back seat. "You getting sick?"

"I'm fine," I say, through the wire mesh. I'm sure there's payment for liars, somewhere.

A year into Mom's illness he took us to a fair that came to

town. I know he had to force himself, distracted, worrying about her. She wanted us to have memories that weren't all about sickness or being scared.

SHE MADE HIM TAKE US. He tried his best. Back when he had a "best". I know he had to force the smile on his face. Until we came to the shooting gallery, but he couldn't hit the target, just kept trying and trying. Artie, nine at the time, said, "it's okay, Dad, I don't want the bear, I just want mamma." Rick cried then, thought he could hide it, pretend everything was normal, with his armor sinking. But he built it up again, thicker than ever. And when he did, he forgot to invite Arthur or me in.

We pull off the highway and onto the roadside. The North Woods in all their majesty stand at our right, an unlikely setting for something so awful about to take place. Even if the wild is cruel.

The team pulls over. There're three patrol wagons filled with about eight cops in each. This is a big deal. The helicopter hovers, scouting the area, and circles back a few times.

I grab a breath when I get out of the police car. The air is damp and heavy with fog. An orange stream lifts through layers of dark blue, as sunrise pushes back the night.

Phil Cox, the Sheriff of Warren County, comes from behind a group of officers. I sink my fists deep into my pockets. Another shiver.

Rick stands in a huddle talking with a few of the officers and the Sheriff. Before long, we're on the move. We take the turn that leads us into the woods. Mr. Spence is ahead of the pack. We pass Teller's Ridge and kept going.

The team stays together, all guns are out and ready.

We meet the rim of the ravine. I peer over the very spot we fell from. Now, with the clarity of daylight, I see how steep it is. We could have easily been killed.

The others in our troupe have their ropes and pulleys in place ready to take the officers down. One, two, and three, they slide. More follow. I hook myself to one of the pulleys and slide down, kicking my feet against the rock and stones, while rubble falls with me.

We gather again and trudge on. Walking until we come to the general area where I'm sure Griffin and Paul Spence found us.

I see the rows of pine trees, but which tree covered Artie and me from the bear? Mr. Spence announces that we're in the general area where he found us. The stream flows underfoot. We're close.

He tells the officers he knows of a cave cluster about a mile from here. We walk on; over branches and fallen trees, under birdcalls, we follow the stream.

Eventually, we're at the area I do recognize, the small clearing with low shrubs. The low shrubs where Gunther picked wild berries for us to eat, the berries I wouldn't touch from his tarred fingers.

"Come, Jackson!" Rick calls me over. He sets up ten men around him while more gather. Sheriff Cox points and maneuvers his men into separate directions. They move quickly and hide out of sight.

I follow on Rick's heels. Some officers stay ahead of us. He suddenly turns to me. "Look, once we find the cave, we're going to surround it--and I want you to go with Spence." He nods to Mr. Spence, who's behind me. I turn to him and acknowledge Rick's words. Dressed from head to toe in gear, he looks almost comical, for a half-second, before reality clubs itself over my head.

"So, listen," Rick says. "Are you listening? This isn't one of your video games, Jackson. This is the real world."

"Yes, of course, I'm listening."

"Soon as we surround the cave you're to get back. Back to marker 4." He nods to Mr. Spence.

"Where?" I have no idea where marker four is.

"Just follow me, kid," Mr. Spence says.

We're being waved ahead. I follow Rick and Mr. Spence, beyond the boulders.

I recognize the pit of bones. The deer entrails still linger in the air. Rick turns to me. "Is this it?"

I nod, once. He waves us back. Mr. Spence tugs at my shirt and I follow him out of sight, behind the trees.

The SWAT team surrounds the cave. One of them tosses tear gas inside. The cave is under siege. I brace myself, expecting the old man to come crawling out on his hands and knees. I'm about to retch, the trees bend and wave, the sky whirls. Jackson, keep it together. There's no running from this.

"Come out with your hands over your head," the Sheriff yells through the bullhorn. "You have thirty seconds. Or we're coming in!

Smoke rolls out of the cave. But there's no sign of Gunther, no response.

Maybe he planned it that way, took off, knowing Artie and I would lead the police here. Or maybe the cave is set to blow? Sherriff Phil counts through the bullhorn, "Five...four... three...two..."

Nothing.

The team ambushes the cave, at light-speed. I keep flinching expecting an explosion—or gunshots. Chaos rattles from inside and echoes out.

"Jackson—you and Paul—Back—NOW!"

Mr. Spence grabs my shoulder and rips me away.

Rick thinks the same thing. Maybe a bomb is set to go off in the cave? Noise clashes against the mountains. Every bang amplifies as they ripped through Gunther's stuff, tossing large bucket drums, and mechanical parts out into the clearing of bones. The old man's supplies become scattered, pages of books flap in the wind, his medical supplies, food supplies, pots, and pans, fly out of the cave at rapid speed.

They find his guns.

The bomb expert comes out of the cave and gives his signal. All is clear. I watch from behind the trees with Mr. Spence. Rick goes in with the Sheriff.

Within minutes, Rick comes out of the cave. Covering his mouth and nose, and holding the rolled-up drawings, he heads over to another officer. Shakes his head, and looks in my direction; his crinkled eyes catch mine. He's tired. Deep crevices between his brows are harsh in the early light, making him appear a hundred years old.

Where's the old man gone? Did he send us here as part of a trap, while he sets a bomb off at another location? Why not? Most of Warren County's police are here.

Rick is standing next to me, and Mr. Spence.

"We can go, Jackson. Your work here is done." He turns to Mr. Spence. "Looks like a lot of bomb-making supplies, the usual stuff, and a deer carcass. Smells like hell in there. I got an address from an envelope, a Mrs. Cornelia Antwerp on Albatross, the other side of North Woods. Looks like he gets disability checks sent there. The Sheriff is sending his men over to check it out."

Then he says to me, "Let's go check on Arthur."

By the time we get to the hospital, it's near 2:00 in the afternoon and way past lunchtime, because we stopped at the precinct in Neumanville, first.

I miss Artie, and worry, although Brianna did say she'd go and stay with him. He must be bored out of his mind waiting for us all morning, and anxious to hear what happened. Rick assures me he'll be out of the hospital soon.

He makes a stop on the way to Artie's room and winds up waiting for the microwave to heat a package he's pulled from the vending machine. He tells me to go ahead.

I open the door to Artie's room and sitting next to him, is a sandy-colored, clean-shaven man. I half recognize him wearing a corduroy jacket and playing chess with Artie. The rat-tails are gone. He looks younger. He looks smart, like a professor in his jacket, and he isn't surprised in the least when he turns his head. "Hiya, Jackson."

But I am.

My mouth is tight, held closed preventing me from a cordial smile. I'm stunned, actually. How dare he sit there, as if nothing's happened?

"Gunther's really good at chess." Artie laughs. "Better than me." Artie's the highest-ranked player in school.

"Where's Brianna?"

"Oh, she went to get burgers from Sam's Shack."

I try and hold my panic down, with Rick about to walk into the room any second. "Our father's down the hall," I tell him.

"You know," Artie says. "Gunther used to work at this hospital. Everyone knows him here."

"Um, Dad's down the hall, the lieutenant—and he's about to walk in any second. We just had a steak out at your cave."

"I know Jackson, the helicopter alerted me. I expected as much, with you two high-tailing it out of there. I saw that the two of you discovered my drawings, and naturally, you'd tell the authorities. Who'd of thought your father was a police officer? What luck." He shakes his head.

I detect something. A fever of fear rises on my skin, the prickly alert tells me in its extrasensory way that something very bad is about to happen.

"My home's been ransacked, my supplies, my books, all my drawings, and my work. It's impossible to stop the dominos from falling. Now I'm homeless. I'm simply glad I could get one book out of there and bring it to Arthur." He stops talking to me and makes his move on the chessboard. "Check."

"What are you going to do?" I ask. "They found an address for a Cornelia Antwerp. Who's that?"

"Cornelia's my mother. But she's very old, and not getting around very well. I'll check on her, soon as I finish this game."

"But he doesn't have to know it was you. He'll be looking for a deranged old man with dreads. You're like someone else, now."

The door opens behind me.

"Hey Arthur, how you feeling?" Rick holds a tray, piled with plastic-wrapped vending machine sandwiches. "Who's your friend?" He turns to Gunther.

But Gunther doesn't look up, not until he says, "Checkmate." He smiles at Artie and stands.

"My name is Gunther Antwerp. You have two good boys here, Mr. Bower. They remind me of my son, especially that Arthur, sensitive, aware, and very smart. Both very smart." Gunther glares at me.

Rick's expression is not one of acceptance, and he doesn't return the greeting. He stands there, without a drop of sympathy on his face, for the man in front of him holding his hand out.

Rick sets the tray down.

"Is this the man who had you holed up in the cave?"

I want to say no, he's a completely different man, and looking at him now, he is. And he's changed his mind. Didn't go through with the bombing. Doesn't that count for something? I also want to say he fed us, and wrapped Artie's foot, he kept it dry. He helped us.

"What are you doing here?" Rick asks, stern, reserved, and in true cop-like stoic-ness.

"I came to check on Arthur," Gunther answers, like a long-lost family friend.

Rick flinches.

But Gunther has more to say. "I was worried when the boys left during the night, wounded and maybe lost in the woods. I saw them recognize the two men that found them. And seeing as this is the only hospital for miles . . . "

Artie's face becomes white as if he might hurl. We watch the two of them in a faceoff, happening right in front of us. Rick stands in his uniform; his hand drifts near his gun and wavers there—a signal to Gunther?

"Look," Gunther says. "No harm's been done. Your son, Arthur, convinced me to call the whole thing off, even if my reasons had merit. He's right, I couldn't allow my son's death to be followed by more death, and like Artie said, my war with the State is with the State, alone." He winks at Artie. "It would destroy Anatole's name. That was my son's name, Anatole Antwerp." A halo of sunlight frames Gunther's silhouette from behind.

"I can have this place surrounded in two minutes," Rick says.

I already notice Rick's hit the red button on his pager. His right hand hovers over his gun, the other extends in front of him. "I have to take you in for questioning, Mr. Antwerp. You can tell the precinct your whole story."

"I don't think I can go."

"You have to, you're under arrest."

Before I see it happen, Gunther lifts Artie from the bed and pulls a pistol out from under his jacket. "You'll let me go," Gunther says, "and I won't hurt this young man, but as you know accidents do happen."

Artie doesn't seem scared now. His face is relaxed. But maybe it's the medication they gave him?

Artie and I both know this is the only way Gunther might get out of here. Rick wouldn't be stupid enough to fire a shot, not with Artie between them.

Rick steps back, allowing Gunther to carry Artie through the door. The guard in front of his room stands at attention and draws his gun. He does not interfere when he sees Rick on the scene behind Gunther.

Gunther keeps the small gun to Artie's throat.

My heart stops. Artie's whispering to him; what is he saying? Where does he think he's taking him? How can he do this? He's a liar and deranged. Artie believed him, and I trusted Artie. But it was stupid, and now it's all over.

He's going to kill him. I stumble trying to keep up and almost fold over. My vision blurs. I don't understand? Why is the old man's doing this?

There're gasps from the nurses and doctors as they pass. Gunther drags the two of them down the hall. My eyes dart from

Rick to Gunther to Artie. Each of their expressions is fixed in time, fixed in my mind, memories that'll haunt me for years.

Rick's weariness shows in his slow movements. His exhaustion layers across his face and hangs his body low; after a night of lost sons, compiled by the fear of losing one again from blood poisoning, and now this. He fights to remain focused.

Artie's face pleads with Rick to release Gunther. I know what he's thinking. But that isn't going to happen. Things are about to get worse.

Gunther's eyes are clear; he seems renewed. Maybe the old man did want a new life maybe Artie helped him. Artie has that way with people, especially animals, and Gunther's been transformed from an animal into a human.

But I fear for Artie now, because accidents do happen, and Gunther's about to meet with the entire police force of Warren County in the parking lot.

I have to get closer... I have to say something to Gunther and stop him.

Why'd he risk his chance at a new life by coming back to the hospital? He already knew Artie was safe after his first visit.

If I could somehow scoop Artie up, or distract Gunther, but that's stupid too. There're about twenty patrol cars outside with armed officers, barreling down on a single target. Any one of them could miss.

Rick holds his gun straight ahead. Gunther steps backward, looking behind to make sure no one sneaks up and keeps walking until he reaches the double doors.

A flood of sirens and black-clad riot police swarm the parking lot, insects in a hive, a single unit with one objective.

Rick keeps his pistol stiff and steady. Their eyes lock.

I run behind a sofa in the lobby and watch. I can't get close enough. I don't let my eyes leave either of their faces.

Where will he go? What's his plan? Artie's face moves somewhere, between wonder and terror. One small misstep from Rick, or the others, and it's over. Someone would be killed.

Brianna's outside. She's holding a couple of white Sam's Shack bags, near the officers. They've told her to stand back. She sees me through the glass. "Jackson, NO!" She's shaking her head. They've told her to stand back. She's scared. I've never really seen her scared before. Not like this. Then she sees Artie. She calls his name and drops the paper bags to the ground.

The old man stands between the two glass doors. Between enter and exit. He speaks to Artie. Artie smiles.

Gunther has to know it could be over for him in a second. Of course he knows, and now he'll be responsible for Artie's death, too. I'm sure his little speech to Artie, was something along those lines. If he goes back inside, he'll have to face our father.

There's nowhere to turn.

Gunther moves through the electric doors, holding Artie close. He's surrounded by a dozen patrol cars. The sun must block his vision because his eyes half close.

Sheriff Phil is on the scene. Rick holds his focus on the two of them and follows a few feet behind. "Stand back, Jackson," he shouts, when he passes me near the couch.

Gunther says one last thing to Artie and lets him go.

Artie runs to a patrol car, Brianna hugs him.

I watch from inside the hospital, through the wall of glass, ready and prepared to duck behind the couch again. Brianna mouths the words, "I love you." In those words, a power swells inside me: the power of hope.

Gunther lowers his gun slowly to the ground. He puts his hands on his head. What is he doing? He takes a step forward, the first step that moves him away from the glass doors, and two steps toward the patrol cars. He surrenders.

A single gunshot rings out. It's the Sheriff.

"NO!" Artie screams. Brianna pulls him back.

Another shot hits, and another. Gunther's body slams against the brick wall from the force of the bullets. More explode throughout the parking lot, plastering him upright like a rag doll.

"Stop it—Stop! You're killing him! It's not loaded!"

"Hold Fire!" our father yells.

Artie runs to the old man.

They've stopped. Artie drops to the ground next to him. He's slumped against the building, covered in blood. Artie's not moving. He hovers over Gunther, and there's not a sound from the crowd. Not a sound from Artie. I can't see his face; his curls cover him.

I walk outside, and over to him. No one stops me.

He's holding Gunther's hand. Rick stands above us. Gunther's eyes open. "Watch your boys," he croaks. "... Never let them fight a war that isn't ... theirs to fight." With that, he shuts his eyes and turns away. The paramedics come. They announce he's dead.

I search for Brianna; they won't let her pass. She's standing behind two police officers. Crying. I want to tell her I never stopped loving her. I was only angry.

Angry with myself, for not wanting to move on and be at peace with our decision, or let her go where she needs to be. A decision we made together.

Rick reaches down to lift Artie, but he won't let go of Gunther's hand. Not until he pries each finger off, one by one. He pulls Artie fast against his chest and

holds him. Holding him longer than he has in years. Burrowing into Artie's neck, he grapples at the curls on his head as if Artie could still slip away.

Our father's shaking, trembling, his entire body rocks in agony. His wails rise around us and into the clouds. Artie hides his face in his chest. I come from behind and hug them both, and let loose, and cry in a way I haven't since Mom died.

Gunther lies at our feet. I swear he wears a half-smile. The paramedics pick him up and lay him across the stretcher. They cover his face with the white sheet.

There are no words. But Artie's cries won't stop. The agony he's held in for years explodes and flows into an endless river. My pain and my heartbreak join his river and stream in unison. Brianna's above me, her hand gentle but firm on my shoulder. She doesn't say anything. I stand up and hug her.

Allowing the fear and the worry and regret to dissolve. When I pull away from Brianna, I release the breath I've held too long, suffocating, until a glimpse of what could still be taken away from us became clear.

Rick asks her to please stay at the lodge, at least until we've finished at the station. Mr. Spence and Griffin come around and help us into a patrol car. Brianna says she'll wait for us at the lodge.

I watch the paramedics finish loading Gunther Antwerp into the ambulance while our father sits between us. His arms wrap our shoulders and he pulls us in tight as though he'll never let us go. Not this time.

He cries silently. Says sorry, over and over, apologizing for every wrong word he's said, the guilt he's kept hidden, and for failing us.

He releases everything but holds onto us for good.

THE END

ACKNOWLEDGMENTS

Originally published by Leap Books, 2016.

It truly takes a village to write a book. From the very first inspiration to the finished product, many have helped bring *The Unmoving Sky* into the world. Thank you to the following individuals who without their contributions and support this book would not have been written:

My editor at Leap Books, Judith Graves, for her faith in bringing this story into the world and to my son Aeon, eleven years old at the time, demanded I finish this book after reading the first pages.

Thank you to all my first readers, Jeff Chen and Dana Edwards from my incredibly supportive writer's group, MG Beta Readers, that grew into a blog: Kidliterati. Thank you to both of my sons, for testing my resolve endlessly and ensuring I remember how to fight for what I love. A heartfelt thanks to my BFFs Tania, Nidhi, Patricia S, Patricia C, and Isabel for your encouragement years ago, to take a chance with this writing thing. Thank you to my husband and partner, Alex— none of this would be possible without your feeding and watering me while I'm in the endless pursuit of perfect sentences. Thank you, Momma, who passed away in 2021, my lifelong example of how to stay positive, no matter what, and how to love deeply and unconditionally.